T0121968

A Journey Forgotten

Emily Noll

iUniverse, Inc.
New York   Bloomington

A Journey Forgotten

iUniverse books may be ordered through booksellers or by contacting:

iUniverse
1663 Liberty Drive
Bloomington, IN 47403
www.iuniverse.com
1-800-Authors (1-800-288-4677)

Because of the dynamic nature of the Internet, any Web addresses or links contained in this book may have changed since publication and may no longer be valid. The views expressed in this work are solely those of the author and do not necessarily reflect the views of the publisher, and the publisher hereby disclaims any responsibility for them.

ISBN: 978-1-4401-5914-5 (pbk)
ISBN: 978-1-4401-5915-2 (ebk)

Printed in the United States of America

iUniverse rev. date: 8/12/2009

Chapter 1

She waited with a heavy heart and teary eyes. The storm of people leaving the platform had reduced to a drizzle, and still the familiar face had not appeared. Disbelief was only natural—she felt that a promise set so firmly should have been unshakeable. She also knew nothing had stopped him except himself. The desire to be free ran too deeply for too long and couldn't be curbed now. She had known this from the first moment they'd met but had fought the knowledge, hoping she could do the impossible and change the leopard's spots. As the long-withheld tears began to trickle down her face, the fog that had remained distant for so long finally gave in and enclosed the valley in its misty shroud. This was just another excuse for pain, just another way to justify an end. Or perhaps it was really a beginning ...

Connor Anderson put his pen down and sat back in his chair, groaning as his back stung with pain. He put his arms behind the chair and pulled himself up, hoping his back would crack and release some of the tension. It remained tight, however, and seemed to be stretching even tighter with his efforts. He gave in and leaned forward over the table, his right elbow sliding across the notepad in front of him and smudging the fresh ink. Connor sighed and grabbed a tissue from the half-empty box on the table in front of him. *It doesn't matter,* he told himself as he wiped the ink off his elbow, *it probably won't amount to anything anyway.* He tore the smeared sheet off the pad and placed it on the edge of the table, the newest addition to a stack of similarly half-filled sheets.

He reached over and picked up what he considered his inspiration—the first-run copy of *Devil's Punchbowl*, his third novel, whose fifty-five thousand-copy press run had earned him a seventeen thousand-dollar advance for novel number four. He turned to the back of the book and looked at his twenty-one-year-old face. His mother often teased him that he owed his sales to the striking photo that showed off his dirty blond hair and his piercing green eyes.

When he'd deposited the advance, he'd suddenly realized that writing was more than just a hobby—it had become a decent source of income, which a writing professor had once declared would be impossible. But now, all of a sudden, he'd run dry.

A writer has it so hard, Connor told himself as he stared blankly at the pile of papers next to him. Writing was an art that was very difficult to master and, he asserted, definitely one of the least appreciated forms. The painter could rely on colors and designs to capture the audience's attention, the musician on notes, and the poet on rhyme. The author depended on words alone to weave a web in which the reader would become completely entangled, immersed in the very figments of the author's imagination and transported away to the mysterious world the author created. Or, as in Connor's case, the reader just became entangled and confused by meaningless nonsense. It was very much like a great recipe—it wasn't enough to just have ingredients and throw them together. The ingredients had to be artfully blended to perfection.

Connor glanced around helplessly for something different to do. While seated at his small kitchen table, which served as his writing desk and was rarely glorified with food anymore, he could look into his living room and lounge. The house clearly stated that he was a bachelor. It contained odd bits of furniture that he had picked up from various yard sales in the area. There was a flowery couch some grandmother had been forced to abandon when her children gave her a stylish, new leather couch for Mother's Day, a comfortable old recliner with holes in the seat cushion that some housewife had hurriedly gotten rid of while her husband was away on a fishing trip, a coffee table that bore the stains of countless cups of coffee, a lamp that hadn't been dusted or polished since 1982, and various other knickknacks. To all these items Connor had added his own touches—junk mail that failed to make it all the way to the garbage can, clothes that were no longer needed, and a Glade plug-in that sat far from any plug but would hardly be able to help the musty smell even if it were affixed in an appropriate location.

Connor's eyes fell on the remote control for his small kitchen TV, and he grabbed at it as if he was drowning and it was a precious life raft. He flipped the TV on and immediately turned it back off, prompted by the small scrap of self-discipline he had left. He reluctantly picked up his pen and threw a sideways glance at the stack of papers next to him.

"What's the point—it's all just bullshit," he said to Ralph, tossing the pen up in the air and watching it bounce off the table and onto the floor. Lying on a padded dog bed just to the left of Connor's chair, the boxer puppy lifted his head at the sound and glanced at the pen when it hit the floor, but he apparently decided it wasn't worth leaving his warm, soft bed and immediately returned to sleep.

"Man's best friend," Connor grunted at the dog. "What kind of friend sleeps when there's trouble?" Either Ralph didn't hear this or decided to ignore it as he remained motionless. Connor grunted once more and turned his attention back to the papers.

Until this last month, Connor had believed that writer's block belonged in the same category as Big Foot and the Loch Ness Monster. Connor had always believed it was a fictitious ailment invented and perpetuated by authors in an effort to make their jobs seem far more difficult than they really were. Writing had always come so easily to Connor that the concept of not being able to write freely whenever he wanted had never occurred to him. When in school he had no difficulty filling notebook after notebook with short and long stories alike. While other students had struggled to catch up on writing that was due three months earlier, Connor had been making the requirements for writing that was not due for another year.

Now that he had encountered the barrier he had once believed fictitious, Connor was immensely frustrated to find that it had many different forms. Writer's block didn't have to mean he had no ideas at all—it could mean he had too many to write down or mean he had plenty of good initial ideas but no thoughts on story development. This last form of writer's block was the one Connor currently wrestled with. No matter the amount of effort he exerted, he produced only small tidbits of stories that went nowhere. They had no real beginnings and certainly no ends, lasting the length of three paragraphs if he was lucky. The brief ideas themselves were not a problem—story ideas quite often bugged Connor until he put them down on paper. However, they usually led Connor on a journey to their appropriate destination, and all he had to do was pay close attention and take careful notes. Now the ideas were piled one upon another like the bitter layers of an onion. Connor was beginning to fear that each layer would be the last, revealing nothing underneath it to account for all his troubles. The pile of paper at the corner of his desk symbolized a month of work—an enigma of unrelated writings that had entered and left his mind in the space of a few moments. While many of his books had written themselves, Connor was certain it would have been easier to pass kidney stones the size of watermelon seeds than make anything out of this current plethora of meaningless nonsense.

Connor pulled the stack of papers closer and fanned through them, reading sentences here and there. "No character development, I guess it *will* be the death of me," Connor mumbled aloud as he continued to flip through the pages. He'd once been told by a professor in college that if anything ever stopped him from becoming a great author, it would be his poor character development. His ability to create exciting and interesting situations in his stories intrigued readers, but to fully enjoy a story the readers needed it to be peopled with three-dimensional characters.

"How are we supposed to sympathize with the emotions of a complete stranger?" his professor had once asked. Connor had shrugged it off at the time. Why did it matter that Katie hated bananas because they were eaten by monkeys and monkeys scared her? Did it change the fact that she would have to be on that red-eye flight to Miami or that the bomb was about to detonate? But now he wondered—what if even *he* didn't know his own characters well enough to write about them?

Connor was suddenly jerked from his reverie by loud banging on his front door. Ralph jumped up from his bed in the corner of the kitchen and barked excitedly in answer.

"Oh sure, *that* gets your attention. Can't give up a moment for your poor, unimaginative master, but a stranger ringing at the door …" Connor sulked. Lifting himself delicately out of his comfortable Italian leather but clearly impotent writing chair, Connor rubbed his face and straightened his shirt. Ralph whined and pawed at the door, obviously distraught that Connor wasn't moving more quickly. Connor held the squirming puppy back as he opened the door. Jim Basken, his editor, stood just outside.

"November 9th, 2010!" Jim announced, pushing past Connor and into the house. Jim had a habit of stating the date as a way of announcing himself, simply because it was a gentle but constant reminder of ever-present deadlines. Connor found this particularly amusing in view of the fact that Jim often erred in his recollection of the current date, as he had done exactly one week ago, when he had incorrectly announced that it was October 31st.

"What's up?" Jim called back over his shoulder as he moved into the kitchen.

"Unnngh …" Connor uttered half-heartedly, closing the door and releasing Ralph. Ralph ran to Jim, jumping up and pawing at the editor's legs. Jim dodged the large puppy paws, dancing his small, five-foot, six-inch frame around the room to avoid an uncomfortable collision with his precious cargo, the sparse island of brown hair on top of his head swaying and moving like a sea anemone in a light ocean current.

"That good, eh?" Jim smiled, placing a grocery bag on the kitchen counter and patting Ralph's head. "I brought you some donuts and coffee. You know—the good stuff you need in order to survive in the morning."

"Not that it'll matter. I feel like I've been awake for fifty years," Connor replied, sinking back into his chair.

"Did you sleep at all last night?" Jim asked, pulling a box of donuts out of the bag and grabbing a glazed one. Connor could almost hear the sound of Jim's hardworking elastic waistband stretching even further in anticipation of the sugary snack.

"Yeah, but I might as well not have. I couldn't possibly have any less energy," Connor said, sinking even lower into his chair. "Here." He handed Jim the stack of half-filled papers from the corner of the table.

"What's this?" Jim asked, swallowing a bite of donut and taking another.

"Odds and ends."

"You're kidding," Jim mumbled around his mouthful of donut as he flipped through the stack, his fingers leaving sticky prints.

"That's all I can get out right now," Connor said.

"This is pretty bad. Tried a cold shower?" Jim asked. Jim had once joked that a cold shower would erase all of Connor's unproductive thoughts and free up his imagination. They had laughed it off at the time, but hours later when his imagination suddenly ran dry, Connor tried the cold shower for fun and was amused to find it worked. Since then, his more elusive ideas were always "caught" in a cold shower.

"Yeah, four times yesterday and once again this morning. The problem is that there are no pesky thoughts to clear away and no great ideas to free up—there's just nothing there at all."

"Here, try these," Jim said, reaching into his pocket and handing Connor a small, clear bottle, half-filled with yellow pills.

"No, I don't take drugs—they give me a bad headache." Connor waved his hand, holding out the bottle for Jim.

"They aren't drugs, Connor, they're vitamin supplements," Jim indicated to the label on the side. Connor turned the bottle around.

"They don't look like vitamins. They look like sugarcoated pain meds." Connor opened the bottle and sniffed. "They *smell* like sugarcoated pain meds."

"Actually, they *do* taste pretty good—like lemonheads. Guess they figured it would help them go down easier," Jim said, his lips curling into a smile.

"Adrenalean," Connor read from the label. He raised his eyebrows and looked at Jim.

"Yeah, I know it sounds stupid, but you'll have to

believe me that it works. Gets that adrenaline pumping normally again. You'll see," Jim nodded eagerly. "We've gotta get you rolling again somehow. Contract's up in a month and a half, and they're starting to get worried you won't deliver."

Connor shrugged. "I don't know how to convince you, but I just can't write what's not there," he said.

"I know, and that's all fine and dandy when you're a freelance writer without a penny to your name, living in some poor excuse for a hovel. But when you have a deadline and multiple financial responsibilities, you've gotta work around it. Anything that pops into your head, write it down."

"What do you think you've got in your hands?"

"Well, maybe there's something in here. You can, you know, arrange them in some order and then you've got what," he flipped through the papers, "a hundredth of your book done. Maybe. I can never tell with these handwritten pages. When are you going to get a computer?"

"Never," Connor asserted, his mind suddenly occupied. What if he played with the small scraps of story for a while? Maybe, like Scrabble letters, they *could* form something if he just got them into the right order.

"I don't know what your problem is with computers. Some loyalty to Shakespeare and ink-stained fingers, I suppose," Jim offered. Connor remained quiet. "Or maybe you think it's lucky."

"Did I ever tell you about Frank Madden?" Connor asked, only half paying attention as his creative mind continued to run on autopilot.

"No," Jim said, looking uninterested. He picked at

another donut, and Connor knew the man's sweet tooth was aching for it while his conscience fought on behalf of his failed diet and cholesterol-clogged arteries. Then Jim's stomach gurgled, and the contest was over.

"Frank Madden was one of the greatest historical biographers of our time. His writing abilities were mind-boggling, so everyone was really looking forward to his first novel. When the novel was nearly complete, his computer crashed and everything was lost. Madden was so crushed that he vowed he'd never write again, and to this day he's kept that promise, depriving the world of his incredible talent."

"What a load of bologna," Jim chuckled, shaking his head as he threw a chunk of donut into his mouth and then brushed crumbs from his shirt. "If you're actually seriously worried about your computer crashing, back the story up on several disks—hell, print it out every day if it makes you feel better." Jim closed the donut box and pushed it away, turning his full attention to Connor. "And do me a favor—save your wild tales for your work because you certainly need it. Every thought you have should be related to your work."

"Hah," Connor snorted. Every thought *was* related to his work. "Do you have any idea what you're talking about when you give me this kind of advice?"

Jim smiled. "Not a friggen clue. But heck, pep talks don't have to be factual. They just have to be peppy, right?"

Connor laughed. "Sure, Jim, I feel *so* inspired I think I just might be able to write this book now. Thanks a lot."

"Yeah, well, I do what I can." Jim put the papers back down on the table. "I'll just leave these here. I figure it's a waste of time to look through them—you probably won't let me publish them anyway."

"Quality versus quantity," Connor mumbled.

"Yeah right. The only problem is your quality is so low in quantity right now that it may as well be nonexistent," Jim retorted.

"Nah, it's worth it when it comes and you know it," Connor said, picking up the papers and straightening them on the table. "Shit, I know they'll come in handy somewhere. Maybe I'll use them for some book about writer's block." He was only half-joking, as his creative mind chose that moment to truly begin to stir.

"Is that what you're going for? Researching writer's block so that you can write about it?" Jim asked. Connor shrugged noncommittally, just in case Jim thought it a bad idea. Jim continued, "I hope you don't mind if I say that while research is good and all, there's such a thing as taking it too far."

"Yeah, yeah, get outta here," Connor waved Jim toward the door.

"Fine, I'm going. But I'll be back for another helpful pep talk in a couple of days." Jim smiled as Connor closed the door on him.

Connor turned from the door, glancing at the bottle of vitamins Jim had left him and snorting in disgust. He'd never been one to take vitamins. He figured if there wasn't enough nutrition naturally available in food, screw it. He'd rather live pill-free and happy for sixty years than swallow endless tablets and capsules every day just to live five years longer. Nonetheless, Jim had seemed quite attached to them. Connor twisted the top of the bottle off and smelled the pills again. They certainly smelled good. If nothing else, at least they would be sweet, and the more he thought about it the more his mouth began to water.

"What the hell," Connor said, dropping a couple pills into his hand, throwing them into his mouth, and grabbing a cup of water. He stopped, rolling the pills around in his mouth carefully. The pills tasted good, sweet but also sour—exactly like lemonheads. Knowing that in a few more seconds the coating would be gone and the pills would taste ghastly, he tipped back the glass of water and swallowed a couple gulps, forcing the pills down his throat.

Connor cleared his throat, pleased to find the pills had not left a bitter aftertaste in his mouth as he had expected. He twisted the cap onto the bottle and then stopped. He unscrewed the cap, grabbed two more of the yellow pills, and threw them into his mouth. He waited a few moments, sucking the sweet coating off, and then swallowed them with a gulp of water.

Ralph barked inquisitively at Connor's feet.

"What's up, boy? Huh?" Connor said, leaning forward with his hands on his knees, his face just above the puppy's boxy brown face. Small black lines above Ralph's eyes, the only black on his entire coat, gave the impression of almost human eyebrows that seemed to dance when he was excited. "Wanna go for a walk?"

"Rowrf!" Ralph responded, bowing his front legs playfully in answer.

"Come on then," Connor said, moving toward the front door. Ralph followed, jumping up on Connor's legs excitedly. "No," Connor said gently, pushing Ralph onto the floor. "Sit," he tried. Ralph bent his back legs slightly but didn't sit down. "Good enough," Connor accepted, pushing the leash halter over Ralph's head and fastening it under his front legs. "Here we go." Connor pulled the front door open and stood back as Ralph ran out and stopped just before the leash went taut. Connor grabbed a sweatshirt off the couch and followed Ralph out, closing and locking the house door behind him. As they stepped off the front porch, they were greeted by a chilly ocean breeze that smelled of wet sand and saltwater.

Connor let Ralph guide the way down their short street and onto the pedestrian trail that ran parallel to the Oregon coastline. To the north, Connor saw the small gathering of buildings that marked downtown Beacon, and he smiled. He had grown up in Los Angeles, California, and when his mother began hinting on his twenty-second birthday that he should move out on his own, he decided that while he wanted to continue living near the ocean, he wouldn't mind a change of scenery and a change of pace. After much debate, a little research, and a scenic road trip, he ended up in Beacon and quickly fell in love with it. It was charming and friendly, and most importantly to Connor, it was quiet and inexpensive. A house that cost five hundred thousand dollars in Los Angeles cost less than two hundred thousand dollars in Beacon and came with much more land. For a young bachelor, and a writer at that, every penny was worth gold and had to be saved just in case … well, apparently just in case the impossible actually happened and he fell impotent as a writer.

A family out for a bicycle ride and heading straight for them caught Connor's eye, and he carefully pulled Ralph back, wrapping the leash around his hand to shorten it. As the family rode past them, Ralph leaped at the bicycles, barking and struggling to break free from Connor's strong grasp. Connor bent and passed his hand over the puppy's soft head, patting it gently. Ralph had been Connor's twenty-fourth birthday present from his parents—a small bundle of fur delivered to his doorstep from the Beacon Pet Shop early in the morning of July 23rd, 2010. Connor obtained this gift through not-so-subtle implications that he wouldn't be half as lonely as he was if he had a pet to keep him company. His mother had responded to this implication with one of her own— that a nice young woman, and perhaps some kids, could keep him company even better than a dog—but she still followed up on his request and made the necessary calls.

As they continued walking, Connor's eyes passed over Ralph's body, mentally calculating how much the puppy had grown in just the last few days. In the three months since his arrival, Ralph had tripled in size, testing Connor's budgeting abilities during the last month as he ate his way through several bags of dog food. Connor's own meals shrank as Ralph's grew, but even this arrangement couldn't last much longer. Connor's latest bank statement told him that he couldn't financially last two more months without some drastic change.

As Ralph discovered something new to smell, Connor turned toward the ocean and closed his eyes, breathing in the salty air and trying to relax. *It's no use*, he thought as he opened his eyes—his money troubles wouldn't go away that easily. He had toyed with the idea of getting a "regular" job for several weeks now and had constantly put it off while he exhaustively weighed all other options. But now he had to admit that there were no other options because he had no money in savings, no money available on current credit cards, no credit score to get a new credit card, no wealthy friends to lend him money, and no assets to sell. He had dug himself into quite a little hole, and he needed to find a way out. As distasteful as it was to subject himself to petty labor for forty hours a week, he had slowly come to the realization that it was this or file for bankruptcy and allow *that* shadow to haunt him for the rest of his life.

Ralph moved on, pulling Connor with him. An elderly couple passed, their hands clasped tightly between them, and Connor smiled warmly as he successfully managed to keep Ralph's paws off their legs. The woman wore a generous amount of fine jewelry (*For a walk?* Connor questioned in his head), and Connor's mind wandered back to money. The next question was rather obvious—where would he work? The places that would be the easiest to get into would undoubtedly be the most embarrassing places to work. He could hear his mother now: "So, how was your day? Make a lot of burgers at Burger-Rama?" However, the less-embarrassing places to work likely required training he didn't have. Getting training meant he would have even less free time for his writing, which was the only thing that would eventually get him out of the irritating drudgery that was a full-time job.

Something had to change, certainly, but Connor found himself more and more determined to push through the writer's block and continue with his passion rather than give it up for a demeaning job in fast food.

A loud pop caused Ralph to stop suddenly in the middle of the sidewalk. Connor spotted the kids first and braced himself as Ralph began pulling at the leash and barking. The kids were in a nearby park, setting off small rockets and shouting with excitement. Ralph clearly didn't care what they were doing—he was probably sure that they were all there to play with him, and he had to get over to them immediately before they disappeared.

"Ralph, heel," Connor said emptily, knowing that the command was falling on deaf ears. Another pop, another rocket, and Ralph pulled more urgently than ever. Just as Connor decided to wrap the leash around his hand again for extra leverage, Ralph lunged forward and jerked Connor off his feet. Connor immediately abandoned the leash in order to focus on catching his balance, and Ralph took advantage of this new freedom by bolting across the street toward the park.

The boys were intent on their rockets and didn't see Ralph until he was ten feet away. As soon as they did see him, one boy shrieked and backed up while the other three clapped their gloved hands excitedly. Ralph accepted their invitations and jumped up on the boys, soaking their faces in puppy kisses and dusting their jackets with his short brown hair. Connor arrived at the park seconds later, pulling Ralph back and apologizing, though it hardly seemed necessary. The boys were grinning widely, even the one who had shrieked, and were happily smothering Ralph with kisses and gentle pats.

"What's his name?" one boy asked.

"Ralph," Connor answered.

"Good boy, Ralph! Good boy!" the kid said, patting Ralph on top of his boxy head. Ralph turned his head up to the boy's hand, grabbing his glove with his mouth and tugging it.

"No, Ralph, drop it," Connor said, poking his fingers into the side of Ralph's mouth to open his jaw. Ralph reluctantly released the glove and jumped up at the boy's face, licking it excitedly. The boy giggled and turned his face, his eyes closed against the onslaught of kisses.

As entertaining as Ralph had originally seemed to them, the boys eventually tired of the puppy and headed back to their rockets. Ralph seemed insulted at this brush-off and barked sharply to let the boys know. His barks, however, didn't return a single glance in his direction, and he whined himself to the ground, laying his head sadly on his paws. Connor took the hint and gently pulled on Ralph's leash.

"Come on, Ralph," Connor said. Ralph reluctantly got to his feet, throwing one more hurt glance in the boys' direction. Another pop, and Connor watched the rocket shoot into the dull gray atmosphere that was Oregon's winter sky. For the first time in a month, Connor's mind caught on something more substantial than a flimsy idea. "Space," Connor mumbled aloud. "Some sort of fragility … or a limit to the vastness of space," he continued. "Ralph, let's go," Connor said, pulling harder. Ralph followed Connor as they returned home, and once through the door Connor fell comfortably into his writing chair and picked up his pen. Ralph, still sulking, crawled onto his padded bed and fell asleep whining.

He had never imagined it would end this way. Of all the problems he had ever encountered, this one was certainly the worst. For the first time in his long life, he felt hopeless. He read the report over and over, as if doing so would erase the words and the gravity of their meaning. Then he looked up, his eyes moving across the splendid night sky. He considered the space he was viewing and suddenly it looked incredibly small.

Chapter 2

It all came down to this. All of his hard work and preparation had been building toward this moment. He reached for the switch and his hand froze above it, motionless on his command. It hadn't occurred to him that this moment would be wrought with so much worry and concern. But it was true. If the machine didn't work, after all he had done, there would be no way to save it. And if it couldn't be saved … a slight moan escaped his lips as he considered the consequences. Like a ray of sunshine poking through dark rain clouds, hope pushed through his mind and he flipped the switch, ready for whatever would happen next.

"Hello?" Connor said lifelessly into the phone that had jerked him out of his nap.

"Wow—you sound so much better," Jim said sarcastically. "Still no luck, eh?"

"Worse," Connor asserted. "I had a great idea yesterday and began writing, and it looked like I was back to my old self for a while. But then something strange happened. Five pages in, right in the middle of a sentence, I completely forgot what I was writing about. The whole story just—poof! And I haven't even been able to write one of my scraps of nonsense ever since."

"Shoot. Well, maybe the pep talk worked and you just need another one. Do you want me to come over?" Jim offered.

"No, I'm going to take Ralph for a walk and see if

some fresh air will do me good. I'll call you later and let you know how things are going."

"Okay. Let me know if you need anything," Jim said. "I'm going to be out of the office for a few hours, but you can leave a message with my new secretary. I'll get it when I check in."

"Sure, thanks," Connor said, mumbling a quiet "bye" and dropping the phone into the cradle. His eyes drifted to the bottle of yellow pills on the overturned five-gallon ice cream bucket that served as his bedside table. "Hmm," Connor said thoughtfully, picking the bottle up. He'd taken some of those yesterday—not ten minutes before his dry imagination suddenly yielded a great story idea. "Nah," Connor rejected, putting the bottle back down and sitting up on the edge of the bed. "Then again, they *are* just vitamins, and nothing could possibly hurt at this point," Connor justified to himself, reaching over and picking up the bottle again. He looked over at the foot of the bed and the Beacon Burgers job application sitting there. "Not yet." He opened the bottle and popped three vitamins into his mouth.

"Come on, Ralph," Connor said, carefully putting the halter and leash on the puppy and grabbing his sweatshirt. "Let's go out for some fresh air." Ralph didn't argue, showing Connor the way as he raced out the front door and onto the sidewalk.

With no kids around to smother in kisses, Ralph walked slowly and leisurely. He stopped abruptly to sniff the base of a light pole, and Connor took advantage of the break by closing his eyes and breathing in the cool ocean air. It was refreshing to have a constant excuse for going outside—it briefly took his mind off the problems at home, though he was sure the procrastination would only make things worse. Why was he having so much trouble? It didn't make any sense to him that he had started to develop a great story idea, perhaps better than any other he'd ever had, and yet he had still been thrown back into writer's block. He grinned as he suddenly thought that perhaps all he really needed was a muse.

"Excuse me?" a gentle voice from beside Connor asked. Startled, he opened his eyes and stepped back. Just in front of him, bending over a wiggling Ralph, was a woman who belonged on a high-fashion runway. She stood five feet, eleven inches tall, with gorgeous long legs. Her wavy red hair, which framed the delicate porcelain of her face, was perfectly contrasted by full red lips and beautiful green eyes. The fact that she wasn't a precise embodiment of Connor's dream woman didn't matter at the moment.

"Hi," Connor answered, perfectly aware of the goofy grin on his face and yet completely unable to suppress it.

"Hi," the woman smiled back and stood to face Connor. "Sorry to have startled you—I was just wondering if you knew where Parker Street was," she asked.

"Oh, yeah," Connor replied, his face falling slightly. Though the idea that she had approached him solely for the purpose of flirting was a bit unrealistic, he still felt disappointed that it wasn't the truth. He forced the smile back onto his face and pointed toward the houses on his right, "It's just over one street, there. I mean, beyond the houses," he added haltingly.

"Really? Well, my goodness," she glanced over where he had pointed and shook her head. "Thank you so much—I've been wandering all over the neighborhood and was about to give up and drive back out to the main road to start over." She bent back down, fondling Ralph's ear. "He's very cute," she said, looking up at Connor.

"Thanks," Connor replied, bending down as well. Ralph was evidently quite happy with the full attention he was receiving, and he flopped onto his side, exposing his soft belly.

"What's his name?" she asked, running her nails gently across his belly.

"Ralph," Connor replied.

"Wolf-counselor," she said. "Neat."

"Sorry?" Connor asked, figuring he had misheard her.

"Ralph means 'wolf-counselor' in Teutonic," the woman replied. Connor remained quiet, his eyes fixed gently on hers. She shrugged and continued, "Names can seem so boring sometimes, so I like to find out what they mean. I don't remember them all, but I did remember this one because it was such a unique meaning for such a common name." Connor still said nothing, and a slight blush rose on her cheeks. "I'm sorry, I'm rattling on, aren't I?" she said, turning her eyes back to Ralph as she stood up.

"No, excuse me," Connor apologized, standing as well. "I just … I didn't know Ralph meant that. I looked at him and thought he looked like a Ralph, that's all. But now that I know what it means," he looked down at the puppy that had also risen and was now dancing around at their feet, "that's neat. My name's Connor, by the way," he said impulsively, extending his hand out to her.

"Basha," she replied, gently placing her hand in his.

"Basha," Connor repeated carefully, squeezing her hand gently before releasing it.

"Yeah, it means 'stranger' in Greek," Basha smiled. "Another one I just happen to know," she added.

"Well, that makes sense, it's yours," Connor said, immediately feeling stupid. Why was it that all trace of decorum and sensibility disappeared whenever he was confronted by an attractive person?

"And Connor …?" Basha asked.

"Actually, I don't know what my name means. I think I looked it up once, when I was little or something, but I've forgotten," he said. "Must not have been too good," he added.

"Maybe you should look it up again—refresh your memory," Basha said.

"I promise I'll do that!" Connor said, a little too eagerly. Basha smiled. They both remained silent for a moment, watching Ralph as he followed a lizard on the sidewalk.

"Well, I …" Basha began, taking a step back.

"You know, Ralph and I are going that way anyway, so if you don't mind, can we walk with you?" Connor asked.

"Sure," Basha replied. Connor stepped forward, joining her as she walked toward the end of the street.

"Do you live around here?" Connor asked, looking over at her profile.

"No, I live in Atlanta. I'm visiting a friend and

exploring some job possibilities," Basha replied, dodging Ralph as he suddenly jumped forward across the sidewalk. Connor gently pulled Ralph back and wrapped the leash twice more around his hand to shorten it. "So maybe I should say, 'not yet.' It's a beautiful place. I can see why my friend loves it. You live here, right?" she asked.

"Yeah, just up the street there a little," he turned, indicating toward his house. He felt Ralph tug the leash, hard, and he was jerked forward forcefully.

"He's a bit strong, isn't he?" Basha asked as Connor pulled Ralph back and wrapped the leash around his hand once more.

"Yeah, he's not exactly the most well-trained dog on a leash, but he has fairly good house manners so I tend not to mind."

"Well, house manners are probably the most important, so I'm sure I wouldn't mind either."

"Yeah, but as he gets bigger I'm starting to wonder if some good training may not be such a bad idea," Connor smiled. He didn't add that with his finances in the shape they were in at present, dog training was probably a half a year away at best. A squirrel darted across the road in front of them, and as if to prove Connor's point, Ralph lunged forward with all his strength.

"Watch out!" Basha cried as she raised her hands helplessly. Connor unsuccessfully attempted to keep his balance, falling forward toward the pavement. He turned his head to avoid hitting it on a fire hydrant but realized he wasn't going to make it ...

Connor's head knocked the side of the hydrant and

he fell forward onto the grass, immediately plunging into the blackness of unconsciousness.

Chapter 3

*As night drew closer, he slowly gained power. It sheltered
and protected him, giving him the comfort and strength he'd
missed. Pain, doubt, fear—none of these existed anymore.
It was as if nothing had ever existed before. Under night's
cloak he was unseen and undisturbed. His freakish features,
so boldly frightening in daylight, were invisible at night. The
darkness was his friend and companion, a freedom that was
infinite and unexplored. He was calm, mystic, and beautiful
in his own way. He was the night.*

Connor awoke suddenly, as if something had startled
him. He was too tired to open his eyes, and he rolled
onto his side to fall back asleep. Something was wrong,
though, and Connor felt himself go cold. He realized
his bed was hard, too hard in fact to actually *be* his bed.
And the extreme quiet was punctuated by an unfamiliar
noise—a steady, far-off humming.

Pushing away the cobwebs of sleep, Connor opened
his eyes to find himself in a room smaller than his kitchen.
The walls were a dark gray metal, dull and non-reflec-
tive. Despite this the room seemed bright, and Connor
noticed two small, recessed lights in the ceiling that were
glowing with a bright white light as if their very watt-
age depended on it. A single small window in the wall
to his right opened onto blackness, allowing Connor's
disorientation to become complete. Connor rolled to his
side and stood up, ignoring the pain that stung through
his entire body. He found himself unsteady on his feet,

and he stumbled back against the wall. A tall man in a dark gray, skin-tight suit appeared suddenly and stepped toward him, holding out his hand.

"Careful, Captain, you are not fully well yet." The man stopped a foot from Connor, keeping his hand outstretched as though Connor might fall and the man's one hand would catch him.

"Where … what …" Connor's voice rasped in his throat, his tongue swollen and dry. He closed his mouth and swallowed hard, but there was no saliva to come to his aid.

"Here, drink this," the man said, holding a glass up and touching a straw to Connor's lips. Connor sipped slowly, allowing the liquid to roll around on his tongue and down his throat. He hoped it was water, though he was almost certain he tasted a small amount of alcohol and a trace of lemon.

"What happened?" Connor asked, his eyes running over the lines of the room again. After this second assessment he decided he was in the most modern hospital room he'd ever seen—the equipment was entirely hidden from sight and evidently very quiet. Though he knew the small town of Beacon couldn't possibly have such a sophisticated hospital, he also knew his present location had to be far from any major city because the stars out his window were incredibly vivid. That left him to ponder the questions of where exactly he was and how bad off was he if it required care at some remote, and specialized, hospital.

His eyes moved back to the man attending him. He realized the man was young—he was practically a kid, his face still scarred with pimples. His sandy blonde hair was buzzed short, and Connor searched his memory to remember whether there was a military base somewhere near his home in Oregon. The kid didn't look like a doctor, though he definitely exuded calm confidence. Connor felt a twinge of familiarity and could swear he'd seen the guy somewhere before. The thought was unsettling, and Connor pushed the glass away suspiciously. "Who are you? What's going on?"

"You have a bit of a head injury, Captain. But don't worry," the kid added when Connor's eyes widened fearfully, "with some rest you should be fine."

"Captain?" Connor mumbled.

"Jackson Leeto. Welcome aboard my ship, *Journey*." Captain Leeto took Connor's hand and shook it gently, his other hand carefully supporting Connor's back. Connor stepped away, his eyes fixed on the small porthole window.

"Your ship ..." Connor wandered closer to the window, staring out into the endless blackness it overlooked. "We're in space ... a ship ..." Connor mumbled, the realization that he wasn't on solid ground turning his legs to rubber. He wobbled, sure he would collapse, but Captain Leeto's arm, strong despite its deceptively small size, steadied him. "Where is my ...?"

"I'm afraid your ship is gone, Captain. In answer to your distress call, we programmed in your coordinates as last reported. When we arrived, it appeared you had already crossed the event horizon and there was nothing we could do. However, one of my crew observed a strange property to this black hole—a sort of anomaly within the anomaly, if you will. In effect, it seemed the black hole was purging itself, or experiencing a reverse-gravity flux near singularity. We remained at a safe distance, watching as the remnants of the black hole closed around your ship and shattered it. Fortunately, the bulk of the hull, where your command station was, separated from the wreckage as a sealed pod and we were able to pull you in."

He stopped and then shook his head. "Quite amazing, well, impossible actually, to be that close to singularity and still intact." When Connor remained silent, Captain Leeto continued, sounding somewhat nervous, "The others of your crew who were also in the command station are all well—they have made themselves useful on my ship at their various posts of expertise. You were the most seriously injured, and we are all glad to see that you are now improving."

"My ship? My crew?" Connor asked, focusing his eyes carefully on Captain Leeto.

"What was left of your ship disintegrated shortly after we brought you aboard. We theorize that your ship retained some pressurization from the black hole, and once we breached the vacuum to release the survivors, the internal pressure was too great for the command station alone and it imploded. Your twenty-seven remaining crew members have been working on plans to re-create your ship's programs to help explain and examine the incident. Once we put into Delphine, you can purchase and get back to the business of running your own ship immediately. Of course, your crew is waiting for your full recovery so you can approve their plans, Captain," Leeto explained. Connor nodded, content with the conviction that this was all a dream. If he just played along it would move forward quickly and eventually dissipate altogether as he woke up.

"Sure, I'll look at their plans," Connor agreed. "Should I follow you to them?" He looked around the walls for a door but could see none.

"I'm afraid Doctor Jahna will not allow that just yet. She gave strict instructions that you are to rest and keep quiet until you are more stable. In fact, she was adamant that I was not to make this visit, but I felt it was my duty to welcome you aboard now that you have regained consciousness and some of your strength. But please, rest here now." Leeto indicated to the wall next to Connor, where the small bed hovered above the floor, its single support arm extending out from the wall.

"And when will we reach ... Delphine?" Connor asked as he carefully pulled himself onto the bed. He expected that the bed might give or move a little, considering its only support looked small and delicate, but as he placed his full weight on the bed he noticed it remained perfectly still. Amazing.

"It's about ten galaxies from our present location," Leeto said. Connor shrugged as if to say, "And?" Leeto continued, "We should be there in approximately thirty-six days. Plenty of time for you to rest." Leeto paused. "Despite Doctor Jahna's orders, I will be sure to stop by occasionally and check on your progress. If there is anything I can do for you, just ask any one of my crew and we will be glad to assist you."

"Thank you," Connor said. "Captain Leeto," he added quietly as Leeto left the room. Connor looked around at the smooth walls and the small window that led into darkness. "What a weird dream," he said as he leaned back onto the bed, closing his eyes and allowing sleep to set in.

Chapter 4

Standing at the foot of the mountain, she turned her gaze up, her eyes following the lines of the mountain to the very top. Her mind raced over the details of the climb, noting that it would be harder and harder to climb as she grew closer to the summit. Could she do this? She questioned herself, realizing she had never attempted a feat of this magnitude before and had no training to rely on for help. She felt the seed of doubt begin to plant itself in her mind, but she quickly yanked it away. She could *do this. And she* would *do this. She forced a smile to her face and began to climb.*

"Uuuggh …" Connor groaned, trying to roll over into a more comfortable position but stopping when his head throbbed in protest. He kept his eyes shut tight against the pain.

"Careful there, Captain," a voice told him. Something cool was pressed to his forehead and he relaxed, sighing. "Better, sir?" the voice asked. Connor nodded gently and opened his eyes, his body jerking involuntarily as he realized he was at the edge of the bed. And apparently still dreaming.

"Bed ends there," the young man said politely, indicating with his hand. He was very young, Connor guessed no more than fifteen, and he too wore a skin-tight suit, though his was a lighter gray color than Captain Leeto's had been. The color looked rich against the boy's pale skin and reflected clearly in his blue-gray eyes. Connor pushed himself up onto his elbows, amazed at the effort demanded by this simple task. His stomach gurgled and he made a face.

"I'm sorry," Connor began but then paused, looking around the bare, unfriendly room. "Is there any way I can get …" he paused again, placing his hand on his noisy stomach. The young man smiled.

"Captain Leeto said you could take dinner in the mess hall tonight. Here, let me help you up." He placed a hand on Connor's right arm and another behind his back, gently pulling him forward. Connor slid his legs to the side of the bed and stood up slowly. "Captain Leeto had these brought up for you," the young man said, holding up a gray shirt and pants set, very much like the one he was wearing. "I hope they are okay," he added. Connor ran his fingers along the smooth fabric and nodded. Maybe these spacesuits were comfortable. And warm.

"Thank you," Connor said, reaching his hands to his shirt and pausing. The young man turned obediently.

"I'll be outside," the young man said, palming the wall. A portion of the wall slid up into the ceiling and the man stepped through, the door sliding back down behind him. Connor smiled—what a cool trick. Connor proceeded to unbutton his shirt, a flannel pajama sort, and put on the outfit left for him. His head ached as he moved around, and he leaned against the bed for support. His eyes searched the room while he dressed. He was trying to find some element from his real life that he had used to weave this dream, even though a growing knot of nervousness in his stomach told him this wasn't a dream. When had he ever had the same dream twice, picking up the second dream exactly where the first left off? His dreams were always vague and nonspecific, but this was very specific indeed, he thought to himself as he moved his hand over the walls, feeling their hardness. Furthermore, he couldn't seem to recall being awake between these two dream periods, something that was a substantial blow to that theory.

As Connor zipped and buttoned his slacks, slightly uncomfortable with the skin-tight fit, he suddenly realized his feet were very cold, something else he was certain he'd never experienced in a dream. Perhaps the idea of being cold, but never genuinely feeling cold. He tried to recall if the young man who had just left had been wearing shoes. Was this a shoeless community or had the young man just forgotten to provide them for Connor? Connor moved toward the wall the young man had exited through and was startled by the sound of the bed disappearing into the wall behind him. With the bed out of the way, a small container on the floor was uncovered. Connor bent down to it, feeling for a lever or button to open it. As his palm fell flat on the top surface, the container beeped and opened, revealing a pair of brown loafers. Connor steadied himself by leaning against the wall as he slipped the shoes onto his feet.

His feet now on the way to warmer temperatures (which did nothing for the knot in his stomach), Connor turned toward the "door," eyeing the wall suspiciously. There were no markings anywhere on the wall—no buttons, no levers—nothing to indicate how he was supposed to get out. His eyes fell upon a faint handprint, so he placed his hand over it gently. The door opened immediately, sliding up into the ceiling.

The young man was waiting, and he nodded as Connor stepped out into the corridor. "This way, Captain," he said, moving forward. Connor followed him down the corridor as it curved gently to the right, and as Connor watched the walls he noticed occasional inconsistencies he assumed were doorways. Another spacesuit-clad crewman appeared out of one of these doorways and nodded at Connor and his escort as they passed. Connor's escort tipped his head slightly and continued on down the corridor.

Just as Connor began to think they were coming full circle and would end up right where they had started, his escort stopped suddenly before a doorway and palmed the wall, stepping through into the room beyond. Connor followed him and was immediately greeted by loud applause.

The room they now stood in was much larger and much brighter than the one they had left, the walls a lighter-colored metal and the ceiling dotted with far more lights. The room contained two long rows of tables placed end to end, each row seating about fifteen people. All were dressed in rich blue spacesuits, and all were smiling at Connor, their hands raised in applause. Startled, he smiled and nodded as best he could under pressure and moved down the center aisle behind his escort.

"You look well, Captain," a woman said as Connor passed.

"Very nice to see you, Captain," a man said emphatically. Connor nodded, continuing past them. At the end of the aisle, his escort stopped before an empty chair and indicated for Connor to take it. Connor smiled politely and sat down at the head of the long row. All eyes in the room were on him, and for a terrified moment Connor thought they expected a speech from him. He wished someone in the room would make a noise, anything that would divert attention from him. Hell, even a burp or a bit of flatulence would be welcome.

"To the captain!" someone called out suddenly, and the entire room filled with cheers. Connor sighed with relief and nodded politely, smiling. One thought occupied his mind.

Who am I?

Chapter 5

It took one sentence and one moment to tie his stomach into a tight knot. One sentence out of her mouth, delivered as matter-of-factly as a weather report or a summary of the day's events. The sentence he had hoped never to hear, its meaning one he had hoped never to encounter. Not with her. Not after all they'd been through. Not now. Not ever. But she had opened her mouth and said it, and in that moment he knew his life would never be the same.

Captain Leeto escorted Connor to the captain's quarters after dinner, and Connor was glad to get away from the crowd in the mess hall. While the meal of roast beef and assorted vegetables had been delicious and welcome to his empty stomach, dinner had made Connor feel sneaky and dishonest. Not only did it appear that he was a spaceship captain, but he was evidently a very highly admired one. His entire meal had been steadily interrupted by individual crewmembers coming up to him, shaking his hand and thanking him for saving their life, apologizing to him for the loss they had all suffered, sympathizing with him for his injuries, and pledging themselves to further service under his command.

As Connor reviewed the events of the past hour, he felt he was the undeserving recipient of far too much praise. The fear of being found out haunted him regardless of whether or not this was actually a dream, because very few people responded well to being tricked. He was reminded of the time when he and a friend tricked a lonely old widow into believing that Connor's rabid dog was on the loose. The terrified woman had called the police, and Connor's parents had spent two hours explaining that their dog wasn't rabid and wasn't loose. Connor had been grounded for a month and was forced to apologize sincerely to a woman who smelled of mothballs and Bengay. If that was the response to an eight-year-old's harmless joke, what would an entire crew of adults do to a twenty-four-year-old captain-imposter? If he was dreaming, it seemed more likely that he would imagine his dream woman and very comfortable situations, not a roomful of strangers and the terrifying on-the-spot position he'd been in for the last hour.

"I'm sorry," Captain Leeto said as he palmed open the door to his quarters and indicated for Connor to step in. "I imagine it was quite hard for you to see the losses you have suffered." He followed Connor into the small sitting room and indicated to a chair. Connor sat down, impressed with the luxury present in the dark mahogany desk and shelves, the fabric art wall coverings, and the soft Oriental rug. He almost couldn't see the cold metal walls for all the embellishments. Captain Leeto took a seat behind the desk and swiveled his chair toward Connor. "Doctor Jahna said it was still too soon after your injury for you to be inundated with noise and conversation. However, your crew had become very disheartened, and I know that seeing you in good health did them worlds of good." Captain Leeto held out a cigar box, but Connor shook his head, wondering how on Earth one could smoke in space without causing explosions.

"No, thank you," Connor said politely. "Doctor

Jahna saw me?" he asked after a moment. Captain Leeto nodded.

"Immediately upon your arrival, and every day since."

"While I'm sleeping, I gather," Connor said. Captain Leeto nodded.

"Yes, you have been sleeping quite a lot."

"Is that …" Connor stopped himself, feeling a little hot under the collar. He was going to ask if it was normal procedure for doctors to examine their patients while they were unconscious (and therefore unable to guard their own physical privacy) but thought it might sound like he was openly attacking Doctor Jahna. Connor was in no position to attack anyone, least of all someone he hadn't even met. Furthermore, if unconsciousness was the state he was in 90 percent of the time, his choice was unconscious checkups or none at all. "What was her diagnosis?" Connor asked instead. "Because I don't remember exactly," he added truthfully.

"You have a mild concussion and some minor trauma-related amnesia," Captain Leeto said. "Doctor Jahna is very pleased that you have no permanent or severe damages or injuries."

"I'm sorry, no permanent injuries? I've got a thorough case, not minor, of amnesia here. I think that's pretty severe and permanent," Connor said sharply, immediately regretting it. He'd gone ahead and impulsively attacked the doctor in spite of himself. Captain Leeto shifted in his chair, his body rigid as if fending off a physical attack.

"Doctor Jahna assures us your amnesia is acute and temporary," Captain Leeto replied understandingly.

"And how long is temporary?" Connor asked meekly, trying to recover his lost composure.

"She believes you will slowly regain your full memory over the next few months. By the time we put into Delphine you should be in pretty good shape—just some unimportant details left to recover. That's not to say certain details will not always remain in the dark for you, but Dr. Jahna is certain that your most important, functional memories will be restored. In the meantime, you have access to all of our facilities, and you are free to rest and recuperate in any of our recreation rooms. I guess I should get you a map." Captain Leeto rummaged through a desk drawer and then leaned forward, handing Connor a small device. Connor took it and immediately pressed his thumb to the center of it, releasing a small, three-dimensional map of Leeto's ship. He paused, wondering how he had known to do that. *Because everything is touch-related here*, he assured himself. The hologram hovered above the device, and Connor couldn't resist the feeling that he looked rather like the space-obsessed geeks he had made fun of in high school. They had always been fiddling with little gadgets like this, pretending to make very important decisions as they walked around in robes with serious expressions on their faces. Connor figured he was supposed to rattle off some specs on the ship now and act knowledgeable about any evident hyperdrive modifications and so forth. Connor's lips curled in a smile. Captain Leeto interrupted his daydream, pointing to the hologram.

"As you can see, *Journey* is a 540LS. It's not exactly the same as your ship, but it is quite a basic design and fairly simple to make your way around in. If you do happen to get lost, just palm into the security program and the personnel on duty will assist you. Is there anything else I can do for you?" Captain Leeto finished. Connor felt that though he was trying to be polite, Leeto was clearly stressed by the extra attention Connor and his crew demanded and desperately needed to get back to his regular duties. Again, Connor was reminded of someone else. He stared into Leeto's face for a moment, but there was nothing there to help his memory.

"Actually, do you happen to have any paper, and perhaps a pen?" Connor asked. Captain Leeto reached into his desk drawer, and after a few moments he pulled out a small notebook and pen. He handed them to Connor.

"Anything else?"

"No, thank you." Connor stood, arm outstretched. Captain Leeto took it and shook it firmly. "I really appreciate your generosity and hospitality."

"You're very welcome," Leeto said warmly. Connor turned and palmed open the door, stepping into the hallway.

"Captain," a woman walking down the corridor said, coming to a stop before Connor. She stood as tall as him and gave the appearance of being all legs, long and slender. The tightness of her dark blue uniform didn't look binding or restricting but rather played out the beautiful curves of her body. Her dark brown hair fell several inches below her shoulders and looked as though it had just been styled at a professional salon—it was shiny and full of the body most women only dreamed of. With the contrast of her dark hair, her blue eyes seemed even more shocking, and they were fixed on Connor's eyes. *This is more than a stunning woman, this is my dream woman. I know her*, he told himself with complete certainty, though the realization presented some interesting questions he refused to address. Instead, he smiled warmly and opened his arms, implying a not-so-subtle request.

"Officer Aislinn, hello." To his utter relief, Aislinn accepted his invitation and pressed herself close to his body, bringing with her a wonderful scent of vanilla and sugar. She stepped back suddenly, and Connor could see she was embarrassed.

"It's good to see you, Captain," Aislinn said, her eyes at Connor's feet. "I'd better get back to …" She left the sentence dangling in the air for a moment before turning and hurrying down the corridor. Connor remained in the same spot for several minutes, listening to the pounding of his heart as he tried to hold onto the sweet scent still hanging in the air.

Chapter 6

The saddle creaked as he cinched it tight. The bridle was wet with morning dew, and his gloves darkened as he clasped the reins and threw them over the horse's neck. The early morning sun had begun to peek between the barn's narrow slats of wood, and his heartbeat quickened in anticipation. He gripped the horse's mane firmly and mounted, adjusting the stirrups for comfort. With a gentle squeeze and calm hand, he guided the horse away from the barn and into the open desert. The heavy dew on the tall weed grass tickled at the horse's hooves and he pulled his legs up, prancing and begging to be set off. Instead, he was pulled to a stop, waiting as they did every day. She appeared suddenly, around the low hill to their right, galloping at full speed away from them. He kneed his horse urgently, following in her dust as his horse struggled to keep pace. A small kick brought another short burst of speed, but it wasn't enough. She rounded another small hill and disappeared from sight. He came around the hill seconds later, but it was too late—she was nowhere to be seen. A small patch of white on the desert floor grabbed his attention, forcing his eyes downward. It was nothing more than a single desert rose, virgin and beautiful in the warm morning light.

Doctor Jahna was waiting for Connor the next morning when he awoke. The slow and gentle pattern of waking was jolted off course when he realized there was someone in the room watching him. She smiled gently, most likely in an effort to set him at ease, but Connor cringed at her stare. She was not an attractive woman—her bushy eyebrows and hint of mustache made her far too masculine. Her black hair was coarse and disheveled, looking about as welcome as a handful of dry straw. She was exactly the sort of person whose features Connor would grossly exaggerate in one of his stories, just to get a rise out of his readers.

"Good morning," Doctor Jahna said, her voice raspy and low. Connor nodded distractedly as he pushed himself up on his elbows and sat up. He was suddenly aware that she was directly in front of the door and blocked his only way to put any amount of distance between them. Doctor Jahna remained quiet.

"Morning," Connor managed to push out. This was accepted as an invitation, and Doctor Jahna approached the bed.

"Captain Leeto told me you seemed suspicious of my whereabouts and … methods … since I had only examined you while you were unconscious." Doctor Jahna remained close by, but she did not move to examine him. "I decided to wait a bit longer this morning to introduce myself and also to see if you had any questions." Connor nodded. He knew he had questions, plenty of them, but he couldn't remember even one. He realized he was staring and shifted his eyes to the floor.

"I, uh …" he began, racking his mind for anything he could use. To his dismay, Doctor Jahna reached out and placed her hand on his forehead.

"Please don't worry about that just now. Let me begin my examination, and then we can talk afterwards." Connor nodded, closing his eyes and relaxing his body back down onto the bed. He felt her cold fingers on his wrist, and suddenly he was drifting back to sleep.

***

Connor awoke with his head throbbing and a persistent beeping ringing in his ears. He moved his hand to shut off the alarm, but his arm reacted sluggishly and only moved a couple of inches. His hand felt like it was buried under the weight of something heavy, but as he continued to move it around the feeling dissolved away. His eyes were also heavy, like he hadn't had nearly enough sleep. The beeping continued to grow louder and louder, and he moved again to shut off the alarm.

"Connor?" a familiar voice asked. Connor cracked his eyes open.

"Hi, Jim," Connor tried to smile but his dry lips stuck to his teeth. His editor stood over the hospital bed, looking almost fondly down at him.

"Hey, buddy. How are you feeling?"

"Pretty tired. Head hurts a bit too."

"I'd guess so. Man, I didn't realize you were that desperate to escape your contract responsibilities," Jim laughed nervously. Connor chuckled lightly in response.

"Yeah, well, you never know. I could be working on something here."

"Man, I hope not," Jim said, somewhat seriously.

"How long have I been out?"

"Two days now. And don't worry," Jim added as he saw a shadow cross Connor's face, "I've been taking care of Ralph. He's doing just fine, but he certainly misses you."

"Thanks." A nurse entered the room from behind Jim and placed a tray on the counter.

"Excuse me, sir," the nurse began. "It's time for his vitals—can I ask you to step outside?" She waved her hand toward the door, which accentuated how short her arms were. Short but well toned, Connor noticed, as was the rest of her short, sturdy body.

"Actually, I should be getting home before I'm reported missing," Jim said. Connor smiled. "I'll go feed Ralph and take him for a walk. Glad to see you up, Connor. I'll be by again tomorrow to check on you."

"Thanks, Jim," Connor said as Jim stepped out the door and closed it behind him. Connor closed his eyes as the nurse took his hand. He breathed a deep sigh and opened his eyes just as the nurse bent over him, adjusting the pillow behind his head. Her nametag dangled in his face. "Tarika," Connor read aloud. The nurse smiled.

"My parents wanted to name me Star, but they felt it was far too plain. So they found a more unique word that meant Star and behold—Tarika was born."

"It's very pretty," Connor said, remembering the beautiful woman he had met on his street. Basha. She had been educated about names too, he mused as the nurse pressed the cold metal stethoscope against his inner arm.

"Thank you. Now if you'll just sit back and relax I'll get through this as fast as possible." Connor nodded, closed his eyes, and relaxed his muscles. Exhaustion immediately enveloped him and he gave in to sleep.

***

It seemed only a few seconds had passed, but Connor was suddenly very much awake. Something had woken him up, though the room was quiet. Connor realized that was the problem—the room was too quiet. He opened his eyes and panic immediately seized him as his eyes fell on the bare metal walls surrounding him, broken only with the blackness peeking in through a small, round window.

Chapter 7

The waves crashed against the rocks over and over, apparently trying to force their way through. The spray soaked her face with every wave, dribbling the taste of salt down into her mouth. As dusk fell she could feel the cold seeping into her bones, but she refused to move. He had promised to meet her there, and it was the only place she could still feel his touch. Though cold, it was nonetheless gentle, caressing every inch of her pale face. She could smell him in the air, fresh and cleansing as she drew him deep into her soul. A single tear escaped and rolled down her face, marking the line he had often drawn gently with his thumb. She pressed her eyes closed and felt him once again.

Connor forced himself to think, though the dull ache in his head made it nearly impossible to do so. The hospital room, Jim, and the nurse had been very real to him. How could he now be back here, surrounded by smooth metal walls and the dull hum of a distant engine, where things were just as real? Jim had said he'd been comatose for two days—that was about half as long as he'd been up here. Maybe he was comatose again and this was his brain's way of keeping him occupied. He'd never been in a coma before and had never really researched comas. Maybe the dreams in comas were far more real than the dreams people had during regular sleep.

What threw him off was a guilty feeling that he was supposed to know this place. If he was supposed to know this place, he may as well *try* to remember it, he told himself. Now that he had a chance to really look around, he could tell that the room he was staying in was clearly someone's personal space, and he wondered who was giving up their room for him. He moved his legs off the side of the bed and stood up, stretching. The room, while it contained some personal effects, was organized to a point where it almost felt bare. Picture frames were simple and consumed little space in hideaway alcoves, and a small radio-like device stood on a retractable stand next to the bed. Connor reached his hand out to turn it on, wondering what sort of music one listened to in space. A large red button on top of the device looked promising, and Connor pressed it gently. The radio blared to life, too loud to have distinguishable tones. Connor fumbled for the volume control, forcing the music to recede to a whisper. Connor's ears were ringing, but he could finally distinguish the tones. It was definitely not familiar to him, but it was not as different as he had imagined it might be. It sounded like a variation of rock music, something he felt he could relate to.

Connor pulled out the chair, extending its supporting arm from the wall under the desk, and sank gratefully into its soft cushion. Though he felt comfortable with the size of the room, it was still only half the size of his bedroom at home, and it made him wonder how small the crew's quarters were. He decided, rather impulsively, that he would take advantage of his free pass around *Journey* and do some sort of barrack inspection. There wasn't anything he could do about it if the rooms were small, but their small size could make returning to his room feel like entering a palace.

Connor's eyes passed over the pictures scattered about the pop-out shelves in the room. The people in the pictures seemed unemotional and unattached, their expressions vacant and serious. Connor couldn't tell if they were co-workers, friends, or family. The lack of smiles or close contact between them led Connor to believe they were no closer than acquaintances. However, he countered, what kind of acquaintances took multiple photos together and framed them? The backgrounds made it appear the photos had either been taken on Earth or another planet that was very similar. There were rolling hills dotted with gorgeous trees, expansive open fields, and seaside sunsets. Connor's eyes moved to a smaller photo, a bright picture of a small, black dog which was clearly very happy. Connor turned his eyes away, thinking about Ralph. Hopefully Jim would take care of him until Connor returned. *If* Connor returned.

Connor felt it would be wise to convince himself that he was not really in space, aboard a ship destined for goodness knew where, but rather that he was comatose and dreaming this up. Doctor Jahna had specifically warned him against this, however. She told him it was not wise to speculate against a tangible reality in his current state, but in Connor's mind a reality as diverse and unbelievable as the one he found himself in was not a reality at all. It was not just the change of location that bothered him about this reality—it was obviously a change of time. Space travel of this nature and to this extent was just not yet possible in Connor's time.

As if he needed to disprove his own theory, Connor reached out his hand for the table beside him and placed it flat on the surface. What was this, if not real? Had objects ever been so clear and so solid in his dreams? He couldn't remember if they had been, but it seemed unlikely. He raised his hand to the side of his head, gently rubbing a sore spot there. The bump was also undeniably real and proof that he had hit his head on the hydrant. No, he argued with himself, it was only proof that he had hit his head recently. It carried with it no proof of what he'd hit it on and where. Doctor Jahna would be only too happy to argue that he could've just as easily hit it on a control board in his ship as on a fire hydrant.

And then there was Aislinn, the crewmember Connor had recognized when he left Captain Leeto's quarters. Surrounding his vague memory of her seemed to be memories of massive machines, something he couldn't place in his memories of Earth. This threw Connor into confusion again—was his recognition of her generated by his dream, or did he really and truly recognize her?

Connor finally resigned himself to the fact that if he was dreaming he would eventually wake up. In the meantime, he should enjoy being captain, though the responsibility seemed hideous in view of the fact that he didn't have the faintest clue about how to be a captain. It was helpful that Doctor Jahna had declared him a victim of acute amnesia, as it was a great explanation for his stupidity in regards to commanding a ship and handling space travel.

Connor sighed deeply, only somewhat comforted by that last thought. Even if he still had no idea who he really was.

Chapter 8

Her breath caught in her throat, her unfinished sentence dangling in the air as she strained to hear what she'd long imagined. The deep, low rumble of drums could've just as easily been fictitious as muffled. Her mind raced as she struggled to hear the music she so longed for—fifteen years of hard work were culminating in this final, triumphant moment. Suddenly, as if determined to break through the barrier of uncertainty, the loud trumpet of horns confirmed her deepest wish and she smiled, certain that every struggle to get here had been worth it.

As Connor grew stronger, he resigned himself to pacing *Journey* endlessly, memorizing every turn in every corridor and every door to every room, all the while making notes in the notebook he carried with him. At one point he had thought that getting into the main operation rooms of the ship could prove helpful to him. Every time he wandered into a new room, he was struck by two things—the quiet focus of the crewmembers as they worked, and the strange machinery that seemed to fill the ship. The crewmembers talked mostly in codes, numbers, and letters thrown together much the way police codes were, only these seemed to be fifteen or more digits and letters long and took up nearly 90 percent of the conversation. It was like stepping into a French café—Connor didn't have the beginnings of a clue about what was being said. There were no facial expressions or body language to help him figure the codes out, as the crewmembers held their faces blank and their bodies in a rigid posture.

The machinery itself looked unlike anything Connor had seen before, though certain elements were familiar. The main engine, for example, had spinning wheels and dials over most of its huge mass, making it look almost childlike and comical. A large piston caught his eye, and he thought it looked just like the piston in a car engine, only considerably larger. Another area of the machine had a large rotating drum, which reminded Connor of a printing press he'd once seen. Crewmembers shoved their hands and indeed their entire arms far into the machine, apparently touching buttons and pulling levers that lay deep within. Connor stood watching for an hour, trying to find a pattern to the machine's movements and failing miserably. He had ventured into other rooms but had learned nothing, instead becoming more and more frustrated as unfamiliar codes were used and unfamiliar machines were operated. Connor quickly dropped the pursuit as being worthless. Instead, he reverted back to memorizing the corridors of *Journey*.

Most of the crewmen Connor passed were crew of *Journey*—less frequently they were members of his own crew. It was quite simple to tell which were which. Crewmembers of the *Journey* wore gray spacesuits and were rigid and unfriendly, doing little more than glancing in his direction as he passed. His own crewmembers wore blue spacesuits and were forthcoming in body language and conversation, always evidently happy to see Connor. Connor played these meetings moment by moment, relying on the crewmember's reaction to guide him through the conversation. More recently, Connor had taken to following his crewmembers at a distance after they had parted ways, carefully staying far enough behind to be out of their sight but close enough to hear their conversations. He justified this eavesdropping by telling himself that he was learning about his crew, though so far he hadn't learned much of anything helpful. Whatever they were working on, they weren't talking about it openly in the corridors. He heard mention of Earth several times— the crew spoke of it as a part of human history that they had learned of but had never personally experienced. Apparently it had been a long time since anyone had been there—Earth's solar system was far from their current location. Connor's heart sank at the thought that his home was slipping ever further from his grasp.

Thirty days after Connor first awoke on *Journey*, he was walking down what he had dubbed "the gray corridor" with his head bent forward in thought. From his many wanderings, he had discovered that the gray corridor was the fastest way to get from his quarters to the mess hall, which was located at the center of the ship. It was along this corridor that he ran into the most crewmen and women, so he often avoided it. He was hungry, however, and running across a few crewmembers was a small price to pay for getting a good meal.

"Captain Connor, nice to see you," a voice said. Connor looked up to see two of his crewmen approaching. Connor nodded but remained silent. The crewmen continued past him, rounding a corner and passing out of sight. Connor waited a moment and then carefully followed just out of sight around the curve of the corridor, straining to hear as the men began talking again.

"Anyway, they told me I couldn't have more than one roll with the meal. Not because there weren't enough rolls to go around, but because they just didn't want me to have another one." Connor recognized this as the voice of the shorter, stouter crewman. The man usually smelled stale, like he needed to air out a bit, and his fingers were filthy with grease and ground-in dirt. His posture was less than perfect—he seemed to be frozen in the bent-over position of someone who was forever poking around in an engine.

"That's nothing. I was told yesterday that it was an inconvenience for me to use the john more than twice a day. As if they have limited waste bilges on the ship or something." This voice belonged to the taller, leaner crewman. It was a nasal voice, and Connor almost wanted to step forward and offer the man a tissue in the hope that clearing his sinuses may restore a more normal voice. His thinness was disturbing to Connor—the man looked unhealthy and pale. Despite this, he carried his tall frame well, strutting forward with his neck and head held straight and high.

"No way—john restriction?"

"I'm not kidding. I can't wait until we put into Delphine and get on our own ship again with Captain Connor. He is so much more lenient and level-headed when it comes to the little stuff."

"Hell, he's a regular god compared to Leeto—did you know he even named this ship after himself? Pretty cocky, don't you think?"

"The ship's name is *Journey*."

"Yeah, and Leeto *means* journey."

"Oh."

"Yeah."

Interesting, Connor thought to himself, falling behind the men so their voices turned to incoherent mutters and then disappeared altogether. He pulled from his pocket the small notebook he had already nearly filled and turned to a blank page, jotting down a new note in bold letters. "LEETO = JOURNEY." As he replaced the notebook in his pocket, he forced himself to recall Leeto's face. He was only a kid, and while being cocky might be expected, there was something more there. Connor felt on the verge of recalling something he had forgotten when the thought slipped away, as gently as a leaf in the breeze.

Chapter 9

It was only at the exact moment when things began that he realized he had never truly believed in miracles until now. Knowing about the existence of the very force that gave life did not in itself make him understand it. Now that he was witnessing it, he felt awed and humbled, suddenly aware of something bigger and better than himself.

Connor's introduction to Delphine was a dark gray shadow in the window of his borrowed room as he awoke one morning. The planet was considerably smaller than Earth, and in the dim light provided by a star somewhere behind the planet, Connor could barely distinguish three large landmasses, each about half the size of Earth's Africa. The northern-most mass seemed the origin point of 90 percent of the lights Connor saw on the planet, and he was certain that was where *Journey* was headed.

Planet entry was far smoother than Connor had imagined it would be. He half expected to be pressed back against the wall, sweat beading on his forehead as he watched flames engulf the window. It was, however, about the same sensation as a mildly-turbulent plane landing, with the addition of the sudden and noticeable pull of gravity when the ship entered the planet's orbit and a considerably longer descent to the planet's surface before the ship settled gently onto the platform and the engines powered down.

Captain Leeto escorted Connor off the ship. Both his own and Connor's crew had run off the ship as soon as they docked, and it was likely that they were already enjoying one of Delphine's famous clubs. Space travel, though entertaining and exciting, didn't afford much time for anything else. For this reason breaks were taken full advantage of, and according to several of the crewmen Connor had eavesdropped on during one of his snooping walks on *Journey*, Delphine offered a great variety of entertainment options.

Clubbing was the last thing on Connor's mind. Now, he felt, was when the real test would begin. He could no longer simply pretend to be an observant guest on another captain's ship. As Captain Leeto had pointed out, Connor would now have to run his own. And that, he realized, was only the smallest part of what he had to figure out. Once he got a ship and learned how to run it, he still had to figure out where he was supposed to go and for what purpose.

Journey was docked on a platform approximately two hundred yards above the surface of the planet. To Connor, the port city looked like Seattle, nestled into the curves of rolling hills and low mountains, covered in lush green landscapes, and overlooking a large bay. Landing platforms, like the one where *Journey* had docked, dotted the entire city, as if an overly ambitious architect had liked the look of one so much he'd decided to make a few hundred more. The landing platforms were generally the same size, though a few appeared slightly shorter or taller than the one holding *Journey*. Most were occupied, leaving perhaps only ten platforms empty.

The port city itself was a tangle of skyscrapers in and among the landing platforms. Though many of the buildings were no shorter than thirty stories tall, the landing platforms stood nearly twice their height and dwarfed them into insignificance. Despite his wild fantasies of flying vehicles weaving in and out of airways à la *The Fifth Element*, Connor found there were none, and he could hear the familiar sound of gas engines from the streets below.

As Connor took the elevator down the center of the platform to street level, he wondered how he was going to select a ship to purchase, what he was supposed to ask for, and most importantly, how he was going to purchase it. One thing was certain—asking questions regarding any of these points was sure to get him in trouble. Those were the sorts of things he imagined a captain would know backwards and forwards, regardless of anything that ever happened to him. Maybe it would be like car shopping, and he could just go by specs and general feeling. He certainly hoped so. He had always enjoyed car shopping back home on Earth.

The elevator stopped, and Connor stepped out onto the street, immediately overwhelmed by the familiarity of his surroundings. The street was marked down the center with a wide yellow stripe and bordered on each side by a curb and sidewalk. The few cars he saw in the distance looked a little more like the concept cars he'd seen at the Detroit auto show—beautiful, aerodynamic lines and curves defining the low-riding sports car—than the practical cars that dominated the roads back home. After looking around to gain his bearings, he turned right and made his way toward a large door about fifty yards away, smack in the center of a building that had to be at least a thousand yards long but only five stories tall. Strange, Connor thought to himself, to see such a squat building smack dab in the middle of a city full of thirty-story buildings. Though the street was lined with small advertisement signs for ship dealerships, Connor had decided to take Leeto's advice and visit Infinity Travel.

Connor quickly found that the entry to Infinity Travel was difficult to negotiate. What seemed at first to be a simple revolving door, Connor painfully discovered was not. Instead, he was meant to step into the small white square before the door and wait for the door to swing open around him and gently push him into the store. By the time he figured this out, he was aware of several heads turned in his direction. He strained to hear their mutters, swearing he could hear "tourist" and "idiot" whispered more than once.

"Excuse me," Connor said once he entered the shop. He looked around and immediately wondered if he had the wrong place. The shop was a small room, maybe three hundred square feet, and it was nearly empty save one long counter at the back wall and various posters covering the walls. There were three pocket lights in the ceiling, contributing little light to the windowless room. Behind the counter was a door, and Connor was curious to see what was behind it. The man behind the counter turned at the sound of Connor's voice, a sour look on his face as though he had sucked on a lemon once a long time ago and the taste had remained. "I'm looking for a ship," Connor finished his sentence.

"And ...?" the man asked testily, moving his tall, wiry frame toward the edge of the counter and pushing his glasses further up his nose. As Connor drew closer to the man, he detected the odor of fish clinging to the huge, dark blue coveralls that hung from the man's frame. Connor shrugged in answer. "What kind of ship?" the man asked. His face plainly said "idiot." Connor cleared his throat.

"An Excalibur LS series," Connor said, surprising himself by realizing that he knew exactly what he wanted. He could even see the ship in his mind, and he smiled.

"Five hundred or three thousand?" the man asked, his eyebrows rising in sudden surprise as he flipped through a notebook on the counter.

"Uh …" Connor paused, the smile immediately erased from his faced. This was one he didn't know. He looked around emptily at the walls for some clue.

"I can show you both," the man offered, clearing his throat.

"Yes, thank you," Connor said. The man made a mark in his catalog, and then he looked up at Connor expectantly.

"Captain …?" he asked.

"Connor."

"Connor …" the man said as he wrote. Then he paused, his pen suspended above the paper. He looked up, his face softening and a smile lighting his lips. It was like fifteen years had suddenly drained from his face. "Boy, am I glad to see you," he said warmly. "You and your crew are famous—the first to return after having breached an event horizon! I feel honored to meet you," he extended his hand. Connor shook it firmly.

"Thank you …" Connor raised his eyebrows inquisitively.

"Earowin," the man replied. The cranky older man was suddenly an enamored young child, speaking up close and personal with his hero. A little too close actually, and Connor crinkled his nose against the fishy odor as he gently pulled his hand back.

"Earowin," Connor repeated.

"I'll bet you want another ship just like your old one, huh?" Earowin asked. Connor nodded helplessly. "Well, let's go look at the three thousand models then," Earowin said, turning toward the back door and indicating for Connor to follow him. As Connor stepped through the doorway behind Earowin, he found himself in the largest indoor structure he had ever seen. "As you can see, we are the largest ship supplier on Delphine," Earowin said. Connor nodded, struggling to keep from gaping.

They walked along a platform two hundred yards above the storehouse floor, an enormously deep pit dug into the cool ground below them. It appeared there was no need for air conditioning, just some large fans that circulated the cool air. The floor itself was crowded with starships, easily over fifty of them. Some were enormous—the size of several football fields—and some were very small, roughly the size of small houses. Many stood upright, reaching from the floor two hundred yards below the platform to the ceiling twenty yards above Connor's head. Others stretched out along the storehouse floor, one thousand yards from wall to wall. The platform Earowin and Connor stood on was part of a matrix of platforms throughout the storehouse. They crossed above and around every ship, offering a full view from every angle for prospective buyers. At the very center of the storehouse was a large glass elevator, offering an uninterrupted view of the ships as serious buyers were taken down to the floor for a final inside tour of their ship of choice. And everywhere throughout this huge building were people bustling around in small carts and on foot. Connor's eyes were wide, racing around the room and all it contained.

Earowin turned to Connor. "Any one in particular catch your eye?" he asked. Connor remained quiet for a moment, drinking it all in.

"Are these all LS 3000s?"

"Yes, on this side of the shop," Earowin indicated to his right. "We have fifteen new models this year, and with the ten new models from last year we have every style, size, color, and engine—you name it." Earowin walked along the platform, Connor following close behind. "This one here," Earowin said, stopping and pointing to a large ship below them, "is the same model as your previous one, only it's a couple of years newer. You may have noticed a slight malfunction with the hyperdrive on your model any time you were within five hundred thousand kilometers of any physical mass." He paused, perhaps waiting for Connor to agree. Connor nodded obediently. "They found that the faint gravitational pull was affecting the fluid levels in the hyperdrive and causing a minor imbalance just strong enough to give you a little shimmy. A small calibration later and everything's fixed." He pointed again to the ship below them. Connor remained silent. "Shall we?" Earowin asked, indicating to the elevator. Connor ran his eyes over the collection of ships crowding the warehouse. His eyes alighted on a dark ship pressed into the corner farthest from him.

"I'd like to look around a bit more first. May I?" Connor asked, indicating the ships in front of him. Earowin nodded.

"By all means, yes. What's the purpose of shopping if you can't browse?" Earowin followed behind Connor as he moved along the platform, edging toward the back corner of the storehouse and the dark ship hidden there. As Connor passed more and more ships and drew closer to the corner, Earowin seemed to grow nervous, walking more slowly and clearing his throat loudly. Connor ignored him and only stopped when he stood above the dark ship. Grasping the rail for balance, he leaned far out over the ship, his heart racing as his eyes followed its dark lines. The ship was a streamlined, elliptical shape with two sleek tail fins on either side, looking somewhat like the rocket ships Connor had played with when he was younger. Its dark gray surface appeared to absorb all of the light around it, and yet it also glowed, its smooth, rounded surface seeming to beckon Connor toward it.

"What is this?" Connor asked, turning his head toward Earowin but keeping his eyes on the ship. Earowin coughed and shifted his weight.

"That's the extent of our pre-owned inventory," Earowin said. "It's an older model—a 2224. I'm sure you'll want something newer ..." He turned and stepped forward. Connor knew the man was trying to get him to leave, but he chose to ignore Earowin again, instead staying by the railing with his eyes fixed on the ship.

"Is there anything wrong with it?" Connor asked, relaxing his body to lean against the railing comfortably. Earowin stood stiffly before him.

"Well," Earowin began. He shifted again, shrugging. "No, there's nothing wrong with it per se ..." He paused, indicating to the ships in the main area. "That is, not compared to other 2224 models. But, you see, the new models all have wonderful state-of-the-art navigational features and great inner-ship accessories ..."

"Has it been named?" Connor interrupted, trying to make out the lettering on the hull.

"Yes," Earowin admitted. "It's the *Scarlet Tarika*."

"*Scarlet Tarika*," Connor repeated, pulling his notebook out of his pocket.

"It means red star," Earowin said in apparent annoyance. He moved back and forth on his feet as if he needed to use the restroom. Connor was oblivious, his every thought focused on the ship below as he jotted the name in his notebook, just below "LEETO = JOURNEY". His eyes glazed a bit as he stared at the sheet and he saw one small sentence—"JOURNEY RED STAR."

"Journey in the Red Star?" Connor breathed. "I'll take this one," Connor said with conviction, replacing his notebook in his shirt pocket.

"Don't you want to see the inside first?" Earowin shifted to the left and indicated toward the elevator. Connor knew that Earowin hoped to change his mind as they passed the many ships between them and the elevator, and though he didn't intend to change his mind about his purchase, he decided to humor the salesman.

"Okay," Connor said, stepping behind Earowin as

they headed for the elevator. Unsurprisingly, Earowin proceeded to discuss all of the fine specifications of the many newer ships crowding the floor. Connor nodded politely, only occasionally mumbling "Wow," or "Nice." He didn't want to encourage Earowin, but he also didn't want to completely ignore him. After all, they still had to discuss prices.

Earowin's disposition changed to near apathy when they finally faced the *Scarlet Tarika*. He held his arm out toward the lowered entry ramp at the rear of the ship, silently offering Connor the lead.

As the two men walked the main corridor of the ship, stopping to view the command station, engine room, and captain's quarters, Earowin talked on and on in a monotone. Connor didn't hear a word the man said. His eyes drank in every detail, and he was overwhelmed with a feeling of déjà vu. As much as he loved shopping for large machines (toys, as he considered them), never before had he been so overwhelmed and so certain. He stepped down the entry ramp behind Earowin and turned once more to face the ship.

"You know, if there are certain aspects of this ship that you love, we can reconfigure one of the newer models for you. That way you have the interior you want and the newer specifications you need," Earowin's voice pleaded. Connor wanted to laugh in his face—he sounded so pitiful as he tried once more to push for a bigger sale.

"No," Connor said firmly. "I'm buying this one." Earowin nodded obediently, and Connor wondered if he was thinking that the customer was *not* always right.

"Okay, then let's get you the contract." Earowin

walked back toward the shop, his shoulders hunched forward in defeat. Connor followed, turning and looking once more at the ship as he stepped through the doorway and into the shop.

"Scarlet Tarika," he muttered, and a smile curved his lips. He felt like a kid on a treasure hunt. Maybe these interlacing clues would lead him back to his memory. That is, if this was a real life to be remembered.

Chapter 10

The attic creaked loudly, voicing his lonely sadness as he crossed the floor to the small, hidden door. He paused, his hand over the handle, a small war fighting inside him. He knew the pain he'd fought so hard to erase would only be reawakened, but he couldn't stand the thought of letting her go entirely, no matter the pain it brought. He sighed deeply, his hand pulling on the handle and forcing the door open. It was still there, hidden under a new layer of dust but otherwise undisturbed. He smiled, a painful smile that ached deep in his chest, and he pulled the box free of its dark cave. Reaching in, he freed the small album from its resting place and brought it to his chest, hugging it as though for warmth. As he opened the cracked cover, he finally let go and took a breath, allowing life back in.

Much to Connor's relief, he discovered that buying a spaceship was exactly like buying a car. It was considerably more expensive, but the basics of haggling and paperwork were the same. Earowin tried to convince Connor that the extended warranty and service plan were exactly what he needed, and Connor politely refused, holding his ground as Earowin implied that he was making a grave mistake.

The *Scarlet Tarika* would cost Connor just over five million credits (down from the six million credits originally marked on the contract), and though it seemed obvious he would need financing, he was never approached with discussion on how he would make payments. *I must have money somewhere,* Connor thought to himself as he signed paper after paper, passing them back across the table to Earowin. Contrary to his normal habit when signing big contracts, Connor paused to read a few lines from one of the papers. It noted that the withdrawal for the entire purchase of the *Scarlet Tarika* was approved by the purchaser's bank, which was listed as the Credit Bank of Astica. Connor suddenly felt very special—he'd never before been able to pay cash for a large purchase, and he found it to be very freeing. Clearly, he was in a lucrative line of work.

After what seemed a lifetime, Earowin finally stopped passing papers to Connor. He arranged the stack of signed papers on his desk, tapping them into order and slipping them into a large folder. He then turned to Connor and smiled.

"Alright, now that the boring paperwork is done, let's go get your ship." He stood and indicated toward a small elevator shaft to the left of the warehouse door. As Earowin palmed the door and the elevator opened, Connor took one last look around the small office. He'd never before left a dealership worried about how he was going to drive his new purchase. He turned to the elevator, nodding at Earowin as he stepped in.

"Your approved launch platform is P12, which is very convenient," Earowin began. "The port city has been overloaded lately with the holiday traffic, and it could take a full day to get your ship transported elsewhere. Then you'd have to commute yourself and your crew to an entirely different port, spending time and money. This way," Earowin palmed the door again and the elevator slowed, "is much faster and convenient." The elevator door opened. Earowin stepped out onto the warehouse floor, and Connor followed.

The process of moving a ship from the warehouse to a launch platform was a fast one, considering that it involved the transition of such a large object. A new ship owner couldn't exactly fly his ship out of the warehouse, so instead the warehouse floor underneath the ship operated like the deck of an aircraft carrier, lowering the ship to a sub-level. There, the ship was carefully loaded onto a moving platform and taken outside, where it could be flown to its designated launch platform. Connor watched the entire process with keen interest, nodding approvingly whenever eyes turned his way.

"As you know," Earowin said as he walked Connor up the entry ramp and into the ship for the final move onto the launch platform, "Each ship's CPU begins with basic programming, which can be customized later to the captain's discretion. Of course, a previously owned ship will come in with customized programming, at which point the CPU is erased and reset to basic." Earowin stopped at the top of the entry ramp and turned to Connor. They now stood in the main corridor, an off-white hallway that curved around the outer edge of the ship's upper deck. The entry ramp retracted, and Connor braced himself against the gentle movement of the ship being relocated to its launch platform. "Unfortunately, we found that the customized programs on the *Scarlet Tarika* were structured in such a way that it would likely corrupt most of the ship's basic programming to try to erase them." Earowin caught the puzzled look on Connor's face and smiled knowingly. "Kinda like someone bringing in a tricked-out Lamborghini—it would cost more and possibly damage the car to try to get the car back to its basic design. Why bother, we figured, especially if the new owner may like the changes?" Connor smiled, grateful for the analogy.

"I appreciate that, and I'm sure we'll be able to quickly assess what we want and what we need to reprogram," Connor said, trying to sound as sure as he could.

"As I indicated earlier, there is that small malfunction with the hyperdrive. We can perform that calibration for you here, and you'll be good to go," Earowin offered. Connor wanted to laugh out loud—the final up-sell attempt was so deliberate he felt right at home.

"That's fine, Earowin. I'm sure we can take care of it." Connor hoped he wasn't lying and hoped in the same way that mechanics could adjust cars, his engineers would be able to make small calibrations to the ship's systems.

"Okay, well, I'll leave you to it," Earowin took Connor's hand and shook it firmly. "It has been a privilege serving you, Captain Connor, and I wish you good luck on your future ventures." Connor nodded politely, waiting patiently for the moment when he would be alone with his ship.

Waiting for the dealership pilot to exit before him, Earowin finally made his way down the entry ramp and turned one last time to salute Connor before moving away toward the platform elevator. Connor could've sworn he saw Earowin shaking his head. Connor smiled and turned to walk deeper into his ship.

Connor's initial thought while taking the tour had

been that the ship was incredibly larger on the inside than it looked from the outside. The command station at the front of the ship was very roomy—there was easily enough room for forty people to work comfortably in there. The mess hall was also large but wisely designed to eliminate wasted space. On the lower deck there were enough barrack rooms for all twenty-seven members of his crew, and he was pleased to see that they were slightly larger and more accommodating than the crew barracks on Captain Leeto's *Journey.* The captain's quarters were still smaller than he would like, but he couldn't imagine he would be spending much time in there so he didn't really mind.

Connor wasn't sure how his crew would be alerted to the new ship. However, as Earowin had demonstrated, news traveled fast in a port city, and chances were the crew knew the name of their new ship and its berth almost as soon as he did. The most important task at hand was for Connor to learn about his ship—or figure out a really quick way to jog the memory he'd apparently lost. He stepped into the ship's main corridor and made his way to the command station. He'd watched enough *Star Trek* to recognize the bridge and know which chair must be his, and he was happy to discover that it was infinitely more comfortable than it looked. From this position he was able to see the entire command station, and the sight caused Connor's heart to sink. His eyes moved over the thousands and thousands of dials, levers, and buttons, each one more confusing than the next. There were symbols and numbers next to most, but it may as well have been in Sanskrit for all the good it did him.

Connor stood from the chair and stepped up to the control unit on the bridge. There were fewer dials and buttons here, but he assumed they were far more important. Connor knew it could be devastating to press one wrong button, but he couldn't help it. His hand moved from his side to the control board, and there was only a momentary pause before he let it rest on a large LED screen.

The computer sprang to life, opening a large holographic screen just before Connor's face. He sighed, happy to see a system's check program in lieu of the world's end.

"Having fun, Captain?" a voice startled Connor, and he spun around to see Aislinn standing behind him. Again, Connor was struck by her beauty and how it seemed absolutely perfect in every way. Her long, slender frame and startling blue eyes riveted him to the spot, and he was acutely aware of how he was ogling her. Trying to regain his composure, Connor nodded. Aislinn smiled and stepped forward. "News travels fast in a port city. As soon as I heard about our new ship I decided I should find you," she said warmly. "I figured you would be here."

"Well, I have to, uh …" Connor paused. He had to what? What would sound good? "I just wanted to look over the new ship, get familiar with everything," Connor finished. That sounded okay, didn't it?

"I understand."

"Not interested in staying out with the rest of the crew?" Connor asked.

"No, Captain. I have plenty to do on the ship, and not much of a reason to stay landside." Aislinn smiled again, and Connor found himself relaxing. She could be indispensable to him, if he could trust her completely.

"Your dedication is admirable," Connor tried.

"Yes, Captain," Aislinn acknowledged.

"If you are considering that you may be neglecting your duties, please rest assured that you aren't. I don't expect we'll have a place to get off to for at least another day anyway, so if you have anyone to call …"

"I have no family," Aislinn said gently, shifting her body. It occurred to Connor that this news was something he had known before, and he felt embarrassed. Aislinn shifted again, resting her right hand just above her hip. *She looks like a model,* Connor thought to himself, running his eyes part way down her legs before stopping himself.

"I'm sorry to hear that," Connor responded apologetically, his eyes on the floor.

"It's okay. It's been twenty years, plenty long to adjust," Aislinn said patiently. As he watched a blush rise on her cheeks, Connor found himself staring at her again.

"I'm sorry all the same. I know what it's like to be … estranged from family," he swallowed over a homesick pang that threatened to crack his voice, "It never really heals completely."

"Are they far from here?" Aislinn asked politely.

Connor managed a small smile. She was humoring him. He thought of home, on Earth, as he remembered it. "Yes, very far. Sometimes I wonder if I really remember them at all, or if it's just a dream I've …"

"Conjured up to make yourself feel better about not remembering all the details anymore?" Aislinn finished.

"Exactly."

They stood silent for a few moments, both deep in thought. As if suddenly remembering where he was, Connor straightened his posture and cleared his throat, turning toward Aislinn.

"I was wondering," Connor began, and then stopped. If he was going to do this, he'd have to give up everything to Aislinn. She would have to know every single detail, and then she'd be able to help him.

"Is there ... something wrong, Captain?" Aislinn pressed gently. Connor's eyes met hers, and he was relieved to see only deep concern, no suspicion. Connor hoped that if there was anyone to trust, it was Aislinn. She seemed like the sort of person you would want to confide in. He took a deep breath and jumped in.

"Actually, I need to ask for your help. I was diagnosed with acute amnesia following the accident several months ago."

"Yes, Captain," Aislinn acknowledged, taking a step toward Connor and clasping her hands together in front of her. "Doctor Jahna informed the crew prior to our leaving *Journey* when we first arrived on Delphine."

"She did?"

"Yes, Captain," Aislinn nodded.

"That's good. And did she tell you ... anything else?" Connor questioned.

"Just to expect a recovery period, Captain, during which you may act as though you have forgotten some aspects of your past."

"Aspects of my past—she said that?"

"Yes, Captain," Aislinn affirmed.

"Yes," Connor repeated, clearing his throat. "Well, the problem, Aislinn, is that I'm almost certain that I do not have amnesia of any sort, acute or otherwise." He ran his fingers through his hair, an unconscious attempt to make himself look better for an attractive woman.

"You remember, then?" Aislinn asked, her hopeful blue eyes fixed on his.

"The truth, Aislinn, is that I honestly don't feel like I remember anything at all about this life. The things that I do seem to remember ... well, to be rather blunt I feel they are memories or knowledge from someone or somewhere else, not the pre-accident self Doctor Jahna promises I'm missing."

"I'm sorry, Captain, I don't quite understand what you are trying to say," Aislinn's voice contained the same confusion that was written all over her face.

"Aislinn," Connor paused, "I don't believe that I am the captain you and the crew believe me to be." Connor paused again, allowing this to sink in. Her face remained the same—any change was either slight or entirely non-existent. "The life I remember before several months ago is as a resident of Earth, living as an author in a small town on the northwestern coast of the United States. I remember everything there, including my family, my schooling, my friends, my neighbors, my car, my dog ..." His voice failed him for a moment as he remembered Ralph. Who knew where Ralph was now ... Connor just hoped he was being well cared for. "In short, my memories are limited to that life. I don't know anything about this ship, how to navigate space, or what higher purpose I'm meant to serve as a captain. I couldn't tell you the difference between an ohm and an amp to save my life. Yet here I am, a captain on a space vessel with an entire crew looking to me to make rational decisions as I fight to understand how I arrived here and how to get back to where I know I belong. The only reason I'm telling you this is because I need your help and I couldn't very well ask it without explaining myself." Connor stopped and watched the information sink in.

"You don't remember ... anything?" Aislinn asked cautiously. Connor shook his head carefully. "Not the ship, the crew, the black hole ... *anything?*" Aislinn clarified. Connor shook his head again.

"It seems that some bits and pieces of things, like your name, have come to me in a déjà vu sort of fashion, and while I can't really explain those," Connor paused for a moment to realize how odd those little moments were, "they are few and far between. I've been able to muddle my way through up until now, but now I'm facing the greatest challenge in commanding this new spaceship." Aislinn nodded. "I'm also certain that the crew would quickly become restless and question my decisions and actions more and more as time carried on. I don't know why this has happened, or how it has happened, but I truly feel that if I can just get through this you will find the old, familiar captain restored to you. I just can't do it on my own." Connor shrugged.

"What do you need, Captain?" Aislinn smiled.

Connor grinned at the title, glad Aislinn felt comfortable enough with what he had just told her to continue with the charade anyway. "Thank you, Aislinn. Your help will be greatly appreciated as I try to figure all this out.

For now, I just want to get through some basic questions. Have I been appointed as captain by a commanding authority?" Aislinn's face wrinkled in confusion. "I mean, have I been appointed to this position by a counsel that I have to report to?" Aislinn smiled, shaking her head gently back and forth.

"Your specific captainship is by your decision alone. The only requirement to maintain your position is that you must assist other vessels when they are in distress and document and report any new findings. That," Aislinn added, seeing the concern on Connor's face, "is something I can assist you in doing." Connor smiled and nodded.

"So we are just … exploring space?" Connor asked. Aislinn's face went pale, and Connor's heart leaped into his throat. How could someone so beautiful look more stunning still, even when clearly distressed? The sudden pale tone made Aislinn's blue eyes and full, red lips look even more enticing. Connor forced his eyes away from her face and swallowed.

"Well …" Aislinn paused. "Yes, we are exploring space, but it was within a specific parameter," she finished, stepping up to the computer before his chair and quickly pressing a few buttons. The large window at the front of the command station faded quickly to black, turning the room dark. *Cool!* Connor's inner child shouted. Aislinn pressed a few more buttons, and a map of space came up onto the screen. The screen extended across the entire front of the command station—it was about twenty feet tall and forty feet wide. The individual stations below it were dwarfed by the enormous map, the crew chairs appearing too small for human use.

"Meaning?" Connor pressed her.

"Do you remember anything about black holes?" Aislinn asked, her back still to him as she continued to press buttons. Connor suddenly realized he had been holding his breath, and he sighed.

"Very little—they are imploded stars and have weird gravity properties."

Aislinn smiled and turned to face him. "That's basically correct. The theory of black holes, or frozen stars, is that due to their pull on the time-space continuum, they have a gravitational pull so strong that escape velocity is greater than the speed of light. Therefore, when you pass into the outer region of a black hole …"

"The event horizon," Connor added helpfully, noticing the small pinpoints of dimmed light scattered throughout the smooth ceiling.

"Exactly, the event horizon, you have entered that gravitational field and no escape velocity we are capable of can prevent you from hitting singularity—the center."

"Okay …?" Connor shrugged.

"The belief that the mere existence of a black hole in a galaxy would draw all planets in the galaxy into singularity has long since been dismissed. A black hole, though it has greater escape velocity, is not unlike any other massive form in space. It may pull close objects into an orbit, but it needs more force for that object to pass through the event horizon." Aislinn brought her hands to her hips.

"Yes," Connor answered, more aware of the sweat

beads forming at the back of his neck than the information Aislinn was sharing with him.

"We therefore paid no real mind to black holes, aside from the curiosity that constant study will help satiate. As long as we stayed clear of the event horizon, we found we could pass rather close to these anomalies without incident."

"I see," Connor said. Aislinn paused, her eyes on his. He was nervous and hoped she thought it was because of the inundation of information, not her close physical proximity. She cleared her throat and then continued, slowly.

"Just about a decade ago, a research vessel made a startling discovery." Aislinn stopped again, swallowing hard. Connor smiled slightly and nodded, urging her to continue. She held his eyes, and then suddenly looked away. "The research vessel found what appeared to be the edge of the universe."

"The edge of the universe?" Connor repeated in incredulity, his attention finally completely on the conversation. Aislinn nodded.

"Of course, no one ever supposed that it was impossible for there to be an end or edge, but technology and research seemed to imply that the time-space continuum might be infinite. This discovery violently contradicted all those theories while at the same time introducing new theories about parallel universes." Connor shook his head, his forehead crinkled.

"How do you mean?"

"The research vessel had not come across a finite end to space. It had come across a sort of … advancing barricade," Aislinn motioned with her hands, drawing them out across an invisible line in front of her.

"An advancing barricade of …" Connor's eyes left her face as his mind caught on, "black holes," he finished. "The BHB—black hole brigade, they called it," he remembered aloud. Aislinn nodded, urging him to remember more. Connor seemed stumped, however, and she continued.

"It was the first time they saw a black hole that wasn't stationary but was in fact moving forward, swallowing space and time as it grew." Aislinn moved her hands and the invisible line forward. "And it wasn't just one black hole—it was an endless row of them, one right next to the other. Understandably, this alarmed the scientific community not just because it threw many of their prior ideas out the window but because of the ramifications."

"The ramifications—you mean the fact that it was swallowing the universe?" Connor asked.

"Well, yes, but also its close proximity to one of the most heavily populated galaxies in the known universe." She returned to the computer and pressed a single button, drawing up the image of a spiral galaxy Connor knew very well.

"You mean it was found just outside of …"

"Yes. As you can imagine, most planet populations have simply decided to move now, but our entire grasp of the known universe essentially extends out along the very same parallel as the BHB. We haven't had the time to move much further inward."

"So we're … exploring deep space for habitable planets?" Connor asked.

"Not really. It is theorized that the BHB would eventually wipe those out as well, so it would be pretty pointless to limit ourselves that way. With the knowledge of the BHB, however, came the realization that there had to be a parallel universe, someplace else that time and space was being purged to at least at the same rate that the BHB 'ate' it up. And that was the beginning of the revolution."

"The revolution?"

"Exactly. Space became divided. There were those who accepted the fate of this universe and were resigned to the idea that the BHB would end all life. The Big Bang theory was reexamined, and this was believed to be the ending of one chapter, thereby allowing the next chapter to begin. And then there were those …"

"Who refused to accept so bleak an end," Connor finished. Aislinn nodded.

"We've spent the last decade searching for the perfect antithesis to the BHB."

"By which it ends, so must it begin," Connor muttered to himself. If black holes were eating the universe, it made sense that they too would hold the solution for finding a wormhole to a parallel universe.

"There have been several strong theories surrounding anomalies that have been found, but most have been found unworkable. Only one of these anomalies persisted past all known obstacles, but then it disappeared around the very ship that discovered it," Aislinn said pointedly. Connor indicated toward himself, and she nodded.

"The anomaly we found, it was … different," Connor said. Aislinn nodded again.

"It binged regularly, like the BHB, but it evidently purged regularly as well and held its position in space and time. This worked well with the theory that it, in fact, wormholed to another universe and purged there."

"Well, isn't that the solution then? We just send a probe through and see what happens?" Connor hoped he wasn't stating the obvious. Unfortunately, Aislinn's face told him he was.

"That's what we were attempting when …" She stopped herself, and Connor knew it was silly to ask her to go on. The anomaly Captain Leeto had spoken of, the one Connor's ship had been destroyed in, had disappeared. Regardless of the impossibility of such a thing happening, it had happened. All focus now was on finding another such anomaly, a responsibility he shared with who knew how many others. Aislinn pressed several buttons on the command console, and the star screen faded back to the window, brightening the command station once again.

"Thank you, Aislinn. I understand what we are meant to do now." Connor smiled widely, perhaps a little too widely, and shrugged. "I suppose you'll want to get settled into your barracks room."

"You're welcome, and thank you … Captain Connor," Aislinn said with a smile. As she left the command station, Connor felt like he could read her thoughts. Despite what he had told her, he knew she saw the familiar Captain Connor in him somewhere.

Chapter 11

She knelt in the dewy grass and pressed the palms of her hands against her legs. Closing her eyes, she took a deep breath in and then exhaled, trying desperately to blow away her troubles. Reopening her eyes, she leaned forward, scooping out the wet dirt to make a small hole, aware of the dirt packing beneath her nails as she did so. Using her index finger to measure the depths, she dug many more holes and felt the tension easing off her shoulders. She rubbed sweat from her forehead, feeling dirt cake there, and finally she smiled. Carefully placing the small green bulbs in the holes and covering them gently, she relaxed completely. There was always a chance for new beginnings. Always.

By the time Connor had finished wandering the five decks of the ship and taken a long nap in his quarters, the crew had discovered their new ship's berth and were making their way to the launch platform.

Connor walked out toward the entry ramp and stood in the main corridor at the top of the ramp as the crew filtered onto the ship. Everyone went straight to the barracks and organized themselves—Connor noticed them dividing into small groups and taking rooms quickly and quietly. Within ten minutes of arriving in their barracks, the crewmembers again dispersed, this time to their various posts on the ship. It seemed that less than half the group filtered to places other than the command station, where it appeared, when he walked in, that at least fifteen of his twenty-seven crewmembers were stationed. There were four crew in the engine room, three crew in the dining hall (he wondered how that would work when they had to prep food for and clean up after twenty-seven), Doctor Simon in the sickbay, and the remaining few crew scattered to other posts Connor had yet to become familiar with. Connor was relieved, since anything done without his immediate direction saved him from exposing himself as the ignorant commander he was.

Aislinn was Connor's right hand in the command room, and he couldn't be more relieved. She seemed to have a friendly connection with him that made him feel comfortable around her even in a working environment. Connor was just glad that Aislinn had the skill, knowledge, and authority to essentially run the ship without him. The crew accepted her commands as normal and natural. She was the superior they looked to for direct orders, though they recognized the captain's supreme authority bolstered that. Aislinn knew to discuss all major decisions with him, and that was all he wanted.

Though he was certain of nothing, Connor was fairly sure that the bridge in the command station was the best place for him to be when he wasn't resting in his quarters. Once there, he was acknowledged with smiles and nods from the crew, who then returned to their stations. Connor sank into his chair, but immediately felt uncomfortable and stood up again. He noticed a star map on the control board in front of him and bent over it studiously. It appeared to be a smaller version of the star screen that had covered the command station window earlier. Though definitely smaller, it was still of decent size, being about three feet tall and six feet wide. The map looked like a collage of NASA's Hubble Space Telescope photos he had once seen at a space museum. It was covered with bright colors and swirled clouds against the sheer black of space, looking no more realistic to him now than it had in the museum. It was like a great painter had found a bucket of light and was spreading it across the sky, bending and twisting it until it became the incredible shapes and colors he now saw. He wasn't exactly sure what he was looking at, but he figured that studying the star map carefully would look convincing to anyone who was watching. His eyes fell on a small red dot near the center of the map, and he placed his finger above the point of light.

"Captain?" Aislinn asked. Startled, Connor glanced up and realized that his innocent motion with the star map had automatically caused ship programs to chart a path on the star screen at the front of the command station. Connor coughed and then cleared his throat.

"Officer, can you identify this ..." Connor stopped, hoping Aislinn would fill in what he had left out.

"That is the red star in the Lena system," Aislinn said helpfully, moving closer so that they could keep their voices low and private.

"Red star?" Connor asked, his heart racing. Another clue to his memory, maybe?

"Yes. Like most other red stars, it is commonly believed that the star has long been dead, and we are just now seeing its last light. Until this is confirmed, it will likely remain known simply as the red star," Aislinn explained.

"Scarlet tarika," Connor whispered to himself,

grasping at a thin thread growing in his mind. "Journey <u>to</u> the Red Star?" Aislinn stood waiting for his decision, her fingers poised above the control board. Though he didn't pretend to know anything about the whole subject in which he currently found himself immersed, Connor did know that there was unquestionably a significant distance between their present location and the rosy dot on the star map. "Chart a course for the red star in the Lena system," Connor said finally.

"Captain?" Aislinn questioned immediately.

"Yes, Officer?" Connor asked, his voice low.

"If you care to resume our … I mean, prior to our unfortunate accident with the anomaly on our last ship, our course was taking us over here." She began to map an entirely different system and stopped suddenly, as if she'd been slapped in the face. Her eyes rose to Connor's, and he was sure he saw a shadow of fear cross her face. "Mapping a course for the red star in the Lena system," Aislinn said after a brief pause. She pressed the map screen in front of her several times, stopping when the coordinates were mapped. "Captain, the Lena system is over twenty travel years away in this vessel." Her tone was careful.

"Chart a course," Connor said firmly, his heart pumping in his throat. He wondered if she could see the sweat beading on his forehead.

"Yes, Captain," Aislinn said, nodding to the pilot.

Connor sighed. He knew what she had been thinking. He was suddenly and dramatically changing whatever set course they had been following before the accident. *Is this the dream or the reality?* he asked himself for the thousandth time this week. He couldn't even begin to remember anymore. Nonetheless, he felt some inner impulse prompting him on and on, as if fate was gently guiding him to some predetermined destiny. Whatever was driving him was powerful enough to make him think he needed to follow his instinct. The fact that he had no recollection of the original plans or their cause of establishment left him without any feeling of remorse, regret, or guilt, and though his red star was too far away to hope he could reach it anytime soon, Connor senselessly pushed on, abandoning all the logic and reasoning he had left.

The ship shuddered as it was pushed into an orbit of Delphine and turned toward its destination. As it glided into its flight pattern, it evened out, humming smoothly. Connor sank back comfortably in his chair, mulling over the strange thought that he was somehow going home.

Chapter 12

It was quiet. A little too quiet. Even the sound of the leaves crunching under his feet was muted and hollow. Something was wrong. The tall pines surrounding him stood still, the gentle whisper of the wind through their branches noticeably absent. He glanced through the treetops, searching for a bird, a squirrel, anything moving. There was nothing. Suddenly a loud pop *startled him into jumping several inches into the air. He drew in his breath, holding it in his lungs as though it might be his last. It was here.*

Connor awoke to whispering voices and tried to open his eyes. The message was lost somewhere between his brain and his eyelids, however, and his eyes remained closed.

"*Is it bad?*" a voice whispered. Connor recognized it immediately—Basha.

"*There are some abnormalities, and we're checking into them,*" the other voice answered quietly. Connor was certain he didn't recognize this other voice.

"*Abnormalities?*" Basha asked.

"*Unusual brain activity for a comatose patient. His brain is functioning as though Mr. Anderson is awake. It is not entirely unusual for a comatose patient to act as if in a deep sleep, but to have brain function as if he's awake is a bit …*"

"*New for you?*" Basha's voice sounded haughty, even in a low whisper.

"*Well, yes, but what I'm trying to say is that it is*

indicative of a higher state of body health than we would normally expect in a comatose patient."

"*So you have no idea what's going on?*"

"*I'm not going to lie to you—his test results are fairly puzzling. We are, however, optimistic that he should pull through just fine.*" The voice receded as the last words were spoken, and Connor knew he was drifting away again. "To dream or not to dream," he said silently to himself as a dark cloud enveloped him.

Chapter 13

He shuffled his feet, edging himself closer and closer to the little girl sitting at the edge of the playground. She couldn't have been more than four years old, a full three years younger than him, and yet she seemed to have a maturity that extended far past her four years. Her light brown hair was braided back into a tight pony tail, and throughout the day small strands had broken free, forming a halo around her face that was lit by the sun. Her golden brown eyes and small, pale lips created the perfect picture of innocence, but somehow he knew that she knew more than her appearance gave off, and he wanted so badly to know her and know everything she knew. Because maybe then, finally, he could understand everything that hurt him.

Connor quickly discovered that space travel was far from glamorous. On occasion it was scenic, but by no means was it comfortable or entertaining. The *Scarlet Tarika* was undoubtedly a large ship, but it couldn't have been more than a week before Connor began to feel claustrophobic, just as he had on *Journey*. Connor could step into any room at any time without it being inappropriate or unacceptable, but he wanted to step onto a warm beach or cool mountain trail for a few minutes. He longed to feel the warmth of the sun on his face and the coolness of a breeze in his hair. Space was cold, dark, and lonely, offering none of the things he desired.

"Captain." Connor looked up just in time to nod as a crewman passed him in the corridor just outside the mess hall. The crew mostly bonded together for meals, breaking up neatly into two groups, one group eating while the other held things down on the ship. There were a few individuals, though, who seemed to prefer eating in smaller groups (indigestion, perhaps?) after the main rushes were over. Connor was one of these late eaters.

"What do we have today, Gavin?" Connor asked as he stepped up to the food counter. The chef looked up from stirring one of the food bins and smiled.

"Captain Connor, how nice to see you!" Gavin offered generously. He was a well-fed man, the sort of person Connor liked seeing in a chef's hat, and he was always very cheerful. If he were a bit shorter than five feet, ten inches and a touch rounder than his two hundred twenty-five pounds, he probably would have made a wonderful Santa Claus. His face even flushed in all the proper places when he was cooking over the hot stove, his nose and cheeks turning cherry red. Gavin was rarely in the mess hall when the captain came to meals, but Connor liked to think Gavin looked forward to the times when their paths crossed. "I think we're all out of frogs' legs today, but we reserved some nice turkey breast for you," Gavin chuckled.

"That'll do, that'll do," Connor said. He appreciated these small chats with Gavin more than he was probably willing to admit, even to himself. Gavin reminded him of someone, though Connor was uncertain whom.

"How is that pod collection coming along?" Gavin asked as he spooned a generous helping of turkey breast and gravy onto a plate. Connor smiled, thinking over his special "collection." Fruit was served in colorful plastic pods, sealed for freshness and convenience. Connor had taken to collecting them and was toying with the idea of somehow making a construction out of them. Anything to occupy his free time, since he didn't feel comfortable mingling with the general crew.

"Pretty well—I'm thinking I may be able to start constructing sometime next week. I just have to figure out *what* to construct," Connor replied as he took the plate from Gavin and placed it on his tray. Gavin moved with him along the line toward the salad bar. Since most of the crew had already eaten and left, the serving line was messy with bits of food, forcing Connor to lift his tray several times.

"How about that dream house you're always talking about?" Gavin offered, wiping a towel across some spills on the bar. "The pods should work well for that geometric dome I think." Connor nodded, though he had no idea what Gavin was talking about. Something he'd decided in the past, obviously, when he was someone else who liked geometric domes.

"I don't know, sounds pretty hard," Connor said half-heartedly. He spooned a little salad onto his plate, more for show than hunger. He always wasted more salad than he should, but since he saved the healthy part of his meals for last, he often had no room for them by the time he was done with the main course. Something about Gavin made him feel self-conscious, though, and he knew he would make an attempt to eat some of this salad.

"Yeah, I doubt there's any way to build a geometric dome that isn't a little tricky," Gavin began, "but, man, it sure would look cool," he finished. "You know, I'd never been to Beacon before the revolution, but the photos were plastered everywhere as soon as it was declared the first entirely green city in the country. I'll never forget the row of domes—just the coolest-looking thing I've ever seen. I don't blame you for idealizing one as your dream home."

Did Gavin say Beacon? Could it be the same Beacon Connor remembered—the Beacon back in Oregon? "Yeah," Connor said, his voice clearly betraying his surprise.

"Speaking of which, I should go take my break. Gotta send some telecards back home—have a bunch of birthdays coming up in the family there," Gavin shrugged helplessly. "I wonder how much longer I'll be able to send telecards Earthside. Or how much longer my stubborn family will hold out there," he mumbled as he turned back to the kitchen.

"Oh yeah? Well, have fun, and, uh," Connor looked down at his tray, "thanks for the turkey breast. Looks real juicy." Gavin turned and tipped his head slightly, a gentle salute, then walked back into the depths of the kitchen.

Connor picked up his tray, grabbed a bottle of water from the icebox, and walked over to an empty table. Maybe he would build a geometric dome out of pods. What the heck else did he have to do here, anyway?

Chapter 14

*Never, never again, he promised himself. It was just too pain-
ful, and it never seemed to work out anyway. He wanted to
connect with his patients in order to better help them, but it
seemed that the help was limited and the pain far greater for
all involved. It was useless, he figured, even though he knew
he wouldn't give up. Something drove him, and he knew it
would continue to do so until he finally reached his goal.*

The next day, Connor hurried to the dining room to
discuss the progress of his pod construction with Gavin.
Much to his chagrin, Gavin had left the kitchen before his
arrival, and he was forced to gather his food without the
company of a good conversation. He grabbed a couple
slices of bread off a half-gone loaf and placed some meat
and cheese on the slices, finishing up with sliced pickles
and crisp lettuce leaves. As an afterthought, he stopped
and grabbed a spoon out of the condiment section and
dabbed a small gob of mayonnaise onto the corner of his
plate. As he carried his tray to a nearby table, he noticed
a small group of crewmen and women sitting near the
back of the room. The four of them looked about his
age—maybe they were a group of friends or perhaps two
couples? Impulsively, Connor started to move toward
them and then reconsidered. He didn't know them well
enough, and besides, as their captain they may not be
as comfortable around him. He sat down, pushing the
tray out of his way and placing his plate on the table in

front of him. One of the young women at the other table shrieked suddenly, and Connor glanced over.

"What the heck is that?" the young woman asked loudly, staring down the top of her spacesuit. The man sitting next to her snickered.

"Cleavage, by the looks of it," the man responded, extending his hand for a high five with his buddy across the table. Connor suppressed a chuckle that nearly caused him to swallow his bite of sandwich whole.

"Jesus, Sarish, can't you keep it clean just for ten minutes?" the young woman asked, standing up and shaking out her suit, which did more to jiggle her body parts than it did to get rid of the foreign item within.

"Ah come on, Joya, you love it," Sarish elbowed Joya gently in her side, causing her to flinch and smile.

"Okay, you two, keep it clean," the other woman muttered, making a gagging sound. Sarish laughed.

"It would be really nice to have a little … privacy for a bit," Joya said mournfully, cutting into her steak and forking a piece into her mouth. Sarish nodded eagerly, his hand wandering.

"Absolutely. Get out, stretch our legs, all that," Sarish said. "Ever since the hologram room went down, I've been feeling more and more claustrophobic." They all nodded.

"Oh, man, I know what you mean. I no longer have an excuse for exercising during my free time," the other man said. "I've gained five pounds in the last week. And the way this is going," he indicated to the full plate in front of him, "I'll be up another ten pounds by next week."

"Oh, cut the crap, Jeremy. You never really exercised before. Stop blaming it on the hologram room." The woman shook her head. Jeremy looked across the table at Sarish and shrugged his shoulders.

"She really knows how to lay it on, doesn't she?" Jeremy elbowed his girlfriend, who grunted and then slung some food into Jeremy's lap.

"Good job, Laya, good job," Sarish said, clapping his hands.

"They said it was going to be fixed soon," Joya offered.

Sarish shook his head. "I heard that too, but that's when they just thought the programming was a little short-circuited due to the upgrades that had been made. Apparently they just found out that the entire system is shot—probably just old and needing replacement. That's the problem buying used—you have no idea how abusive the previous owner may have been."

"Well, shoot. What the heck is a rec room without any rec to be had?" Laya shrugged.

"Hey, you're in tight with the captain, Sarish. Why don't you put in a good word for us?" Jeremy's voice was a little quieter, and he probably thought it didn't carry across the room to Connor. All four crewmembers shot not-quite-subtle glances in Connor's direction.

"Yeah, he's right over there, why don't you? Maybe he needs company anyway, and you can ask him to join us and then wiggle it into the conversation somehow," Joya urged, her voice also slightly lower. Sarish shrugged.

"I don't know. I haven't really talked to him much since … you know …" Sarish shrugged again.

"All the more reason to go be friendly," Joya pressed.

"Yeah, okay," Sarish sighed, pushing back his chair and standing up. Connor watched out of the corner of his eye as Sarish approached him. He smiled warmly and nodded.

"Hi, Sarish."

"Captain," Sarish acknowledged. "Would you like to join us?" He indicated toward his table. Connor glanced down at his plate and shook his head.

"Nah, I'm about done here anyway." *What am I doing?* Connor silently questioned himself. This was exactly the sort of friendly group and conversation he longed for, and here he was pushing it away. *Story of my life,* he thought. He had never cultured friendships very well, and he was always worried his friends would find him boring and dump him. So he dumped them first.

"Oh. Well, do you mind if I sit?" Sarish's face looked downcast, as though he'd just been rejected.

"Sure," Connor motioned to the chair across from him. Sarish pulled it back and sat down.

"So," Sarish began and stopped. Connor realized that Sarish was trying to figure out how to start the conversation, something Connor usually struggled with. Though this shared dilemma should have sparked some interest in the conversation, Connor kept quiet. "Have you heard about the hologram room?" Sarish finally asked.

"Yeah," Connor said plainly. He had little understanding of the hologram room's mechanical workings, but he had taken full advantage of it until it stopped working. It had been his only way to experience the ocean and forests he missed so much, and he found it far more interactive and satisfying than he could have imagined. Before stepping into the room, the user would program the system, which had been specially upgraded on the *Scarlet Tarika*, to select the interactive experience of their choice. Normal hologram rooms, from what Connor understood, offered approximately twenty different experiences, from skydiving to snorkeling, racecar driving to horseback riding. The *Scarlet Tarika*'s hologram room, however, offered nearly one thousand different experiences and had been a crew favorite until its recent breakdown. The complete four-dimension experience included sense-stimulators, like the warmth of an engineered sun, the spray of water, and the smell of fresh grass and hot rubber, and it was clearly missed by all.

"Kinda a bummer that it's out of commission," Sarish said.

"Yeah," Connor said. He felt extremely uncomfortable, since he had no idea what had to be done to remedy the situation.

"Well," Sarish said, "I guess I'd better get back …" He let the sentence dangle, unfinished. Connor cleared his throat.

"Alright then," Connor said, standing and picking up his tray. Sarish nodded, raised his hand slightly, and then stood up and turned back to his table. Connor almost swore he heard Sarish mutter something under his breath, something about Captain Leeto. Maybe he was wishing he had stayed on *Journey* with Captain Leeto. But the guy was such an … asshole! Connor was surprised at the thought. It seemed to come out of nowhere and yet he was certain it was true. He'd never had reason to form that opinion, but there it was. Only, he knew it was someone else he was thinking of, not Captain Leeto. Who, then? Connor's mind remained bolted shut, refusing to give him anything in the way of help.

Connor sighed and walked out of the mess hall toward the kitchen. "This just keeps getting better and better," he mumbled under his breath as he pushed his tray through the washing grid and stepped into the corridor.

Chapter 15

He had but one weakness, and it all but destroyed him. It explained every fear, every failure, and every mistake he had ever made. It was always one step ahead of him, and he could never escape it. Worse still, it seemed to be growing more and more powerful, leeching all his strength. The only key to its complete destruction ... lay within him.

Connor's quarters were not nearly as elaborately decorated as Captain Leeto's had been, which suited him fine. The down-to-earth furniture looked well-worn and comfortable, the chairs were deep and cushy, and the desk was sturdy and dependable. Landscape drawings that depicted ocean and mountain scenes decorated the walls, and a single lamp brightened the desk. Connor sat in his comfortable leather chair, waiting patiently for Aislinn.

"Tell me about Captain Leeto," Connor asked as soon as Aislinn stepped into the room. He had called for her to join him in his quarters for this discussion because he much preferred keeping the rest of the crew in the dark regarding his continuing amnesiac condition. Aislinn took a seat across from him, biting her lip as she kept her eyes on the floor.

"Captain Leeto is the youngest captain currently registered in the Starfleet logs," Aislinn began without raising her eyes. "He graduated from the academy when he was fifteen years old and passed the commander test on his first try." She paused dramatically before adding, "No one had done that before, and only one other has done that since. Thanks to a large inheritance, he was able to purchase *Journey* immediately after receiving his captainship, and he has been in space ever since."

"And his reputation?" Connor asked. Aislinn smiled, finally raising her eyes to his.

"Captain Leeto prides himself on being the very best. Becoming the youngest captain only started what has become an endless quest to be better and faster than anyone else. He has done a lot, actually, finding over a dozen various anomalies that were helpful to researchers in understanding the current situation. His discoveries have allowed us to refine our search to a more specific area within the vastness of space. Unfortunately, with that great genius also comes some degree of ..."

"He's an asshole?" Connor asked. Aislinn looked surprised, but nodded.

"Yes, actually," she admitted. "He always claims that he's in it for the greatest good and that he's genuinely happy when others make valid discoveries. The truth is, however, that he often discredits others' discoveries and conclusions, almost like nothing is valid unless he himself is responsible for it." Connor nodded.

"So he doesn't have many friends?" Connor suggested, more as a statement than a question. Aislinn widened her eyes.

"Surprisingly, he actually has quite a few friends. The thing about Leeto ..." Aislinn paused, casting her eyes back to the floor for a moment, "The thing about Leeto is that he appears to be ... oh, what's the word ..." Another pause, and then, "Insecure." This time, it was Connor who looked surprised.

"Insecure?" Connor asked, his disbelief plain on his face. Aislinn nodded.

"It's true that Leeto is very intelligent and devoted to working his hardest, but he seems to rely heavily on approval from others. It's as though he doesn't believe in his success until someone else validates it. Like none of his accomplishments really happened until they earn him awards. Some of his closest friends are other highly successful captains, and so he surrounds himself with success."

"So I should be expecting a dinner invitation sometime soon?" Connor jested lightly. Aislinn laughed.

"I'm surprised he didn't try to get to know you better during our time on *Journey*," Aislinn responded. Connor thought back to how he avoided everyone on *Journey*, even Captain Leeto.

"Perhaps he was a little overwhelmed under the circumstances."

Aislinn shrugged, and Connor took it as an indication that she had nothing more to say. "Thanks, Aislinn, I feel I understand better now," Connor said, hoping the new information would crack through the barrier and reveal who Leeto reminded him of. He was certain that somewhere in the knowledge of Leeto's Earthly counterpart may lay the answer to why he was stuck here.

"You're welcome, Captain." Aislinn stood and walked to the door.

"That one other captain who passed the test on the

first try," Connor said thoughtfully, already suspecting the answer. Aislinn paused. "Who was it?"

"You, Captain."

Connor watched Aislinn leave, a weird feeling gripping his chest from the inside. He felt small and inadequate next to Captain Leeto's many accomplishments, and suddenly he had no idea what he wanted to do.

***

Aislinn had proven far more helpful than Connor had imagined. It was perfectly acceptable for her to run the ship's operations and report progress to Connor as necessary. Connor took advantage of this, growing lazier and lazier about reporting to the bridge and doing so less frequently. Hours rolled into days, days into weeks, and Connor stopped keeping track of time. He no longer believed that he was comatose and dreaming this reality—it was just persisting for far too long. However, without any other memories to fill the void, he was left with an emptiness that was lonely and depressing.

Connor spent most of his time before the window in his quarters, staring out into the darkness it overlooked. Some days he saw a nebula, a supernova, or a distant galaxy, and on occasion he was certain that if he could just reach out, he would be able to touch them. On this particular day, however, there was nothing but the small pinpoints of light from distant stars.

The notebook pages on which Connor had written various passages and his memory clues were soft and thin from constant handling. He had long since lost hope that the words he'd chosen to write down were really clues to his memory, but something kept him from discarding the notebook altogether. After all, it was because of those words that he bought this ship, and something about the ship still felt comfortable and familiar to him. It did not help, however, in discharging the irritation that grew inside him.

Connor had never been a terribly patient person, which led anyone who knew him to believe that he was on an endless emotional rollercoaster. When he was very young, he would startle his parents with outrageous laughter one second and ear-piercing screams the very next second. His mother initially believed that when this occurred he was in pain, perhaps due to a bug bite or a pinched finger, but as she watched him more closely she realized it was just his attitude. He could be content and an instant later ferociously upset about something. When he was content and happy, he was sweet, kind, and generous. When he was upset there was just no telling what he would do, and many a pen cap had suffered the terrible fate of being chewed to bits by Connor's angry teeth.

As Connor had grown up, the sting of frustration became all too familiar. Sometimes he could persist through obstacles for a considerable length of time before growing frustrated, and other times the first setback would be enough to make him want to scream in anger or collapse in tears. School had always been able to push the right buttons on a rather consistent basis, and one particularly difficult assignment in algebra had driven Connor to punching a wall so hard that something had to give. The wall won, and Connor went to school the next day with his broken hand bandaged to three times its normal size.

"Goddamn!" Connor yelled loudly, feeling slight relief as if he was a teapot that had just released some of its steam. He hated feeling disoriented and disconnected, and it was even worse to be stuck in a tin can day in and day out. He leaned over, pulled his loafers onto his feet, and then ran his hands through his hair to smooth it out. A quick glance in the mirror confirmed that the dark circles under his eyes were still very much there, despite his best efforts at sleep. He stepped to the door, glancing down at his uniform once more before palming open the door. "Captain on deck," he muttered under his breath as he moved into the corridor.

***

"Captain has the bridge!" Aislinn called out as Connor entered the control room. The few crew in the command station turned and saluted Connor from their stations. *Where is everyone?* Connor wondered. The crew looked surprised to see him, as surprised as a child would be when his mother walked into the kitchen to discover him on the counter with his hand in the cookie jar right before dinner. Connor nodded to the crew, his face solemn and severe.

"Carry on," Connor said. He thought about asking for a situation report but realized it would probably sound stupid. What was there to be reported on? They were traveling toward a star that was so far away it might as well be nonexistent. In fact, the red glow from the star suggested that it probably *was* nonexistent. Getting a situation report now would be like asking a nationwide marathon runner what his status was after he took one step.

Connor decided to take a seat in his chair and observe. Aislinn proceeded with her work as if Connor wasn't there, busily punching buttons and fiddling with maps and diagrams. Connor found himself ogling her and realized she was incredibly attractive like this—working intently, her dark hair falling forward over her shoulders. A small breeze from a vent blew across her face, pushing her hair back for a moment and revealing a freckle beside her eye. And the smell—like vanilla and sugar. Connor wondered if the old him—the one she remembered—had a thing for Aislinn. Maybe it was mutual. She *had* been really nice to him from the start. Aislinn suddenly looked up, as if she heard these secret thoughts. Connor looked away just before her blue eyes met his, and he instead focused on two crewmen huddled together in a corner of the room. Their postures and low tone implied a very secretive conversation, and when a few devious smiles were shared between them, Connor felt the frustration growing again, pushing his temper's delicate melting pot to the limit.

"Why are they whispering?" Connor asked Aislinn, finally raising his eyes to hers. Aislinn looked back at him as though the question was ambiguous at best.

"I expect it's because they have something private to say," Aislinn replied, shrugging.

"Private or not, they are creating a bit of a disturbance," Connor's eyes were now on the others around the whispering crewmen. Though all appeared to be working normally, they occasionally shot furtive glances in the direction of the two-man huddle. Aislinn didn't see this, or didn't want to see it, and instead watched Connor carefully.

"Are they too loud?" she asked, her forehead crinkled.

"No, they're not. That's the problem," Connor replied, the melting pot beginning to spill over. He stood up and stepped across the walkway, determined to put an end to the whispering at once. Aislinn remained at her post, her facial expression unchanged.

The two crewmen seemed unaware of Connor's presence until he had stopped and stood two feet away from them. They suddenly realized they had been caught abandoning their posts, and by their captain, no less. They turned to move away but found themselves boxed into the corner and unable to go anywhere. They looked like two mice unable to run anywhere except into the trap right before them. They stood about the same height, though there was at least a two-decade age difference between them. They were dressed in the standard dark blue crew spacesuits. Despite the fact that neither man was overweight, the suit clung tightly to the older man's frame and seemed to hang off the younger man. The older man's eyes were on the floor, and the younger man flicked his eyes about as if he were looking for some way to escape. Connor's face remained blank as though he didn't see this obvious panic, and he stood firmly before them with his hands held behind his back.

"Good afternoon," Connor managed warmly, cracking a hint of a smile. The mice remained silent, unsure if accepting the cheese would lure them further into the trap. The younger crewman, Hunter, nodded slightly in response, but kept his lips pressed tightly together. "I noticed that you were busy in conversation," Connor continued, moving slightly to pace before his prey. Hunter, appearing bold, opened his mouth.

"Yes, Captain," Hunter said eagerly. His companion winced.

Connor turned and smiled at the young crewman, trying to decide whether he was bold or ignorant.

"And what, may I ask, were you so busily discussing?" Connor's eyes met Brad's, the older crewman's, but only for a moment. Hunter opened his mouth once more.

"We were discussing drift, Captain," Hunter replied matter-of-factly. Brad nodded in agreement, though Connor could see uncertainty in his dark brown eyes.

"Drift?" Connor repeated, letting the word roll off his tongue slowly. Hunter and Brad nodded earnestly. "Sounds like a very important discussion." The crewmen continued to nod, their heads bouncing in unison. "Any results from this discussion?" he asked casually.

"No, Captain, not yet," Hunter swallowed hard.

"Ah, perhaps it needs more discussion then."

"Yes, Captain."

"Discussion around your workstation so that the discussion can be influenced by your work and vice versa," Connor eyed the instruments behind the crewmen. They looked as though they hadn't been touched in weeks, the buttons and knobs gleaming and shiny. "This sounds very admirable," Connor said, his eyes back on the two crewmen.

"Thank you, Captain," Hunter said, and both he and Brad breathed sighs of relief. Connor smiled greedily, like a hunter who found his trap full. He paced for a moment longer, aware that the eyes of all the crewmen in the room were on him. Finally he stopped, his facial expression set.

"So let me get this straight. You were discussing your assigned posts and duties on this ship, conversation that concerns not only your fellow crew but your captain, and you were doing so in secret?" He allowed an eyebrow to raise in question. Hunter, suddenly not so bold, seemed to shrink back into his uniform. Brad remained silent, and Connor knew he was probably cursing Hunter in his head. But Connor wasn't finished. He continued, his body turned and his voice slightly louder for the benefit of the entire crew.

"I find it interesting that information regarding your work duties could be important enough to be discussed while at your posts, but unimportant enough to warrant normal tones of voice. Now, in the interest of differentiating between two very different subjects, there are matters that are private in nature and need to be discussed privately. Such matters would be those concerning the individual himself, not his post and work duties on this ship. It is only fair and fitting for such matters to be discussed privately in an area where they do not affect or create disturbances for others. A barrack room or the dining room is a good location, as is any space that is not and will not become occupied by others during the conversation. However," he said, turning back toward the two crewmen now on display for the benefit of the entire command station, "Your work station is not now and will not ever be an appropriate place for such whispered discussions. Is that understood?" The two crewmen nodded slightly, sweat beading their foreheads. "Good. Return to your posts," Connor ordered, and he walked back to his own station on the bridge. Aislinn seemed intent on avoiding his gaze as she busied herself with the star map, pressing buttons and making notes in the captain's log. The crew remained quiet for a moment, and the distant hum of the engine and gentle purring of computers was all the noise filling the air until that alone seemed loud enough to permit conversation again. At that exact moment, every crewman in the cockpit began talking again, and Connor sighed so slightly no one heard him.

Chapter 16

As the days passed, Aislinn watched her captain become increasingly restless. He was irritable and sullen, often walking the ship with his shoulders hunched forward and his eyes downcast. Aislinn knew that a minor power failure in the ship's auxiliary system was the perfect excuse, and she wasn't surprised when Connor asked her to set a course for Harbour, the nearest spaceport.

Though she wasn't sure she believed Connor's own explanation, Aislinn felt certain that something in her captain had definitely changed. She also felt certain that whatever it was would only be aggravated further with pushing and prodding. She had become very aware of the fact that Connor was relying on her more heavily during this difficult time, and it was up to her to support him where needed and even defend his actions and decisions when the crew questioned them. At first, the crew had barely whispered about the captain's new lightning quick and fiery temper, but now the whispers had turned to a dull roar and Aislinn found herself struggling to maintain a steady defense. It was easier when the captain was around because the crew knew better than to say anything in his presence, but Aislinn grew to dread the times when she was attending her post without him, which had become more and more often of late. Her own authority with the crew was not enough to explain the captain's increasingly uncharacteristic behavior.

It was not these interactions with the crew, however, that upset her most. It was the reminder that the closeness between herself and the captain seemed to have completely dissolved since the loss of their ship. He still looked at her, of course, but it was always a guilty look, like he had been caught ogling her when he shouldn't have been. She missed the glances that were filled with meaning, the subtle brushes of skin on skin, and the whispered words that gave away deep feelings. She missed the relationship they had begun to nurture, gently stepping into a world filled with romance and excitement.

Aislinn found herself avoiding social situations with her fellow crewmembers more and more. She found it easier to avoid the conversations altogether than deal with the emotions that were aroused. When Sarish called her down to the systems room to review the mechanical systems manifests in preparation for landing, she knew his ulterior motive—since she had avoided him socially, he was attempting to speak with her under the guise of work. In the small room that served as nothing more than a hideaway for just a few of the ship's computer servers, Aislinn sat in a small chair next to Sarish, reviewing manifests and nervously biting her lower lip. Maybe, just maybe, she was wrong and Sarish didn't have anything to say. As Sarish took a deep breath and opened his mouth, Aislinn knew her first instinct had been right.

"What a headache," Sarish said emptily. Aislinn's heart quickened, but she said nothing, hoping to discourage him with silence. Sarish glanced at her and decided that since she was there he may as well continue. "I can't believe he's calling for a pit stop to overhaul the entire system because of a minor auxiliary power failure."

"So?" Aislinn said, trying to make the word a statement

instead of a question and failing miserably. She shuffled through the manifest, suddenly quite restless herself.

"So, what happened to our Captain of old, the one who showed no fear and wouldn't let minor problems slow us down at any cost? Remember how we lost our other ship? That was *his* idea, you know." Sarish placed his papers onto the small table jutting out from the wall and leaned back in his chair as if to get comfortable for a long chat.

"This is a new ship, Sarish, and the captain is just getting a feel for her. I think he's smart to tread lightly." Aislinn kept her eyes on the manifest, her heart aching as she was once again reminded of how things used to be.

"Bullshit." Sarish spat the word out as though it were a bite of rotten food. Aislinn raised her eyebrows in surprise. "Having a new ship never slowed him down before. There's something weird going on here," Sarish said suspiciously.

"Right," Aislinn said, touching the word with as much sarcasm as she could muster.

"You think I'm joking but I'm not. The captain's changed."

"The captain is responsible for a ship that disappeared into a black hole and reemerged shortly thereafter, half-missing, nowhere near functional, and about twenty-five crewmembers short of what it had before entry. That sort of event would change any man."

"No, not like this. I was there too, you know. I saw it. I even held Gurtry's hand those last few moments as he slipped away. But I haven't changed, not like the captain," Sarish said firmly.

"Like what exactly? If you're going to accuse him of change, at least be specific," Aislinn said, placing the manifest down on the table and now fully defensive.

"I can't—the change is so broad." Sarish moved his arms out, gesticulating as if to indicate something big. "It would be like trying to describe the changes in a zebra that had become a lion. It's an entirely different animal, and he's an entirely different person. He doesn't remember half the ship procedures."

"He suffered from acute amnesia," Aislinn said.

"Yeah," Sarish admitted. Aislinn could tell that he was giving up, at least for the moment. She was sure that he had plenty more to say, but he probably realized that telling her was worthless. As officer, she would do whatever was necessary to protect and support her captain. As ... what had she been to the captain personally? Whatever it was, it caused her to guard him even more fiercely, as if doing so helped guard her own emotions. Sarish surely felt that she wouldn't, and couldn't, care about his suspicions.

In truth, Aislinn cared very much about Sarish's suspicions. She knew Sarish had maintained a good relationship with the captain prior to the accident—they had often stopped and exchanged friendly conversation in the passageways. Now the captain acted as though he didn't even recognize Sarish and often struggled to remember his name. Sarish was just another nameless face among the crew, a crew the captain had the power to order around in any way he saw fit. As much as Aislinn wanted to believe that her captain would recover, such an obvious oversight seemed truly impossible for anyone to experience.

Despite her own feelings, Aislinn refused to let Sarish bully her into agreeing that the captain had gone weird. She maintained an air of complete indifference and continued her analysis of the ship's systems in preparation for the mechanical overhaul, flipping through the manifest and tracing her finger along a line of text.

"The computer is reading a high liquid content in the coolant chamber. It could be a manufacturing defect— I've seen it before. An over-zealous worker overloads the coolant during final construction, and it needs to be drained within a few months or it will affect the primary engine systems," Aislinn explained.

"Sure, that makes sense for a new ship. This isn't a new ship."

"Well, maybe the coolant was overloaded at the dealership. Some newbie who wasn't paying attention to his checklist."

"Yeah, okay, but could it affect the auxiliary power systems like we are seeing? I don't remember seeing anything about the correlation of the coolant chamber and the auxiliary power systems." Sarish leaned forward, close over her shoulder, his chest brushing lightly against her back. She wanted to jerk her chair back, away from him, but she restrained herself and only moved slightly to the left. The impulse startled her as she realized she was repulsed by physical contact, especially since she received none from the only person who mattered.

"It's possible but not likely. We're primarily experiencing a disruption in the power for the lights, and the coolant really doesn't have anything to do with that. However, since we are putting in to port for mechanical reasons, we should be alert to and write up anything we find that's out of the ordinary."

"Can the excess coolant be drained in flight?" Sarish asked, looking up from the manifest.

"Yes, there is an over-flow valve that can be opened. The excess coolant can be drained into there and kept in that compartment until we reach a safe dumping location."

"Well, we should go ahead and do that, just to see what happens."

"It's done," Aislinn said coolly. Sarish seemed offended.

"And the auxiliary systems?"

"Still minor failures detected in the system. The main system generator is overworking to compensate, and there is the possibility that it will blow in the near future. A pit stop is really not a bad idea."

Sarish shrugged in annoyance. Aislinn knew that being proven wrong was something that drove Sarish mad. Like a little kid, he would persist until he was right about something, even if it was something he made up. "Well, he could at least choose a location with a better service record."

"He may have other reasons for putting into Harbour that we don't know about," Aislinn said.

"Then his report is incomplete!" Sarish growled, storming out the door of the small room before Aislinn could reply. Aislinn turned back to the manifests, studying them carefully.

"Captain to crew," the speaker rang out. Aislinn stopped reading and looked up at the intercom box. "As you may know, we are docking on Harbour to fully assess and repair our minor auxiliary power failure, the cause of which is not conclusively determined at this time. I'm authorizing a crew leave for forty-eight hours upon arrival. Please return to the ship in a timely fashion, as no lenience will be extended to those crewmembers absent past the forty-eight hour window."

Aislinn frowned. A crew leave for forty-eight hours—there really was something different about this captain. The captain she knew was dedicated and focused during a mission, allowing a very generous leave when all the work was finished. This sudden break in the middle of a mission they hardly understood was confusing and definitely out of character. Although, she posed silently, it may be just the sort of thing to provide a much-needed morale boost to the crew. And that sort of thinking, she mused, was just like the captain of old.

Chapter 17

He walked slowly among the trees, listening to the sound of the wind stirring the branches high overhead. The ground was damp and cool, retaining moisture from the morning's dew. A small, green plant hidden in the underbrush caught his eye. It was twisted and bent, struggling to find the sun it needed to survive. He felt the irony, as he too needed just one thing to survive.

Once they had docked on Harbour, the crew eagerly streamed off the ship. While the spaceport did have the facilities necessary for most ship repairs, it was primarily a tourist destination. The entire planet was a vacationer's dream—white sandy beaches, warm turquoise waters, golf communities, amusement parks, and an endless variety of clubs. The weather was also perfect, not too hot or cold, with the perfect breeze to keep the air fresh. The crew of *Scarlet Tarika* seemed bent on enjoying as much of Harbour as they could over the next two days—all of them except for two people. Connor and Aislinn stood at the top of the ramp, watching as the crew left. Hands were empty, but Connor knew that pockets were full. The crew was unable to keep the smiles off their faces as they stepped out onto the landing platform and packed the street elevator to capacity. Connor smiled slightly, relieved he had been able to bring about a huge change in the crew's morale so easily. He was aware of the fact that his attitude was not sitting well with the crew, and he feared a mutiny was not far off. This leave was sure to earn him some brownie points with the crew. Aislinn clearly seemed to have different feelings, but apparently felt like keeping quiet about them.

"Are you sure you don't want to have some free time?" Connor asked Aislinn, tilting his head toward the landing platform. "You have been working pretty hard lately. You deserve this break," he added warmly, a smile on his lips as he touched her gently on her arm. Aislinn looked startled.

"Well, I …" Aislinn started, placing her hand gently over her throat. Connor wondered what was wrong and then thought that perhaps his closeness had made her uncomfortable. He withdrew his hand, taking a step back.

"Go ahead, please," Connor urged. "I'll be fine alone here, I assure you." Aislinn's face fell.

"Thank you, captain, but no," Aislinn answered quietly. What looked like a forced smile lit her lips briefly before she turned, moving back along the main corridor toward the command station. Connor watched her go, trying desperately to figure out what he was missing. After a moment he shrugged and walked back to his quarters.

A while later, Connor stood on the landing platform as a team of mechanics ran a brief diagnostic on the ship. The team concluded that the failure in the ship's auxiliary power systems was linked to loose wiring in the main engine room. It took them just a few minutes to adjust the wiring and run a successful test on the system. Predictably, the supervising mechanic managed to convince Connor that he should repair the recreation room's hologram program, and that a few minor repairs to the fuel and hyperdrive systems would be to his immense benefit. A few hours (and several hundred additional credits) later, the team left, assuring Connor that all looked a-okay.

Connor walked down the main corridor and into the command station, pressed the ship's intercom button, and called for Aislinn to join him. She arrived seconds later, quietly stepping into the empty, semi-dark room.

"Hi," Connor said informally, nodding as she approached him where he stood at a crew station near the star screen.

"Captain," Aislinn answered politely, and Connor watched her force another small smile.

"Please, sit," Connor indicated in her direction, and she promptly sat at a workstation across from him. Connor waited a moment, and then sighed as he too sat down.

"Is everything alright, Captain?" Aislinn asked delicately as though he were a small pop-rocket that may go off at any moment. Connor forced a smile.

"Not too well, actually, Aislinn," Connor admitted. "I still don't know what I'm doing, and I'm very concerned that I won't figure it out anytime soon." He paused, but the small silence was too much so he carried on. "I need to know that everything is running smoothly. You know … everything."

"Yes, Captain," Aislinn answered.

"If anything comes up that is considered out of the ordinary, you'd tell me, right?" Aislinn nodded at him. "Good. And the crew," Connor paused again, searching for the appropriate words, "I need to know that they are carrying on their full duties, and not becoming distracted."

"Yes, Captain," Aislinn answered.

"I have been hearing rumors, whispers, regarding feelings about my ability to carry on command," Connor clarified. "I need to know that every effort is being made to prevent these rumors and whispers from growing." Aislinn swallowed, and Connor thought she looked nervous. Maybe the rumors and whispers were already more than she could handle.

"If I may suggest, Captain," Aislinn started, "if you reassert your position by being a more constant presence in the command station, this may help divert rumors. Also, you used to make routine speeches about current protocol, and that may help assert your authority." Connor suddenly thought of Captain Leeto.

"Captain Leeto—how did he run the crew?" Connor watched as a shadow passed over Aislinn's face.

"Like a drill sergeant," Aislinn said, and Connor realized she was being polite.

"Thank you, Aislinn, I do appreciate that. So I can continue to count on your help as we move forward?"

"Absolutely, Captain," Aislinn nodded.

"Good," Connor said, still certain that she wanted something from him. If only he could figure out what it was …

***

After a short leave to enjoy one of Harbour's gorgeous beaches by himself for a few hours (it was a relief to be able to get outside for a change), Connor returned to the ship and waited for his crew to arrive. Connor was very aware of the crew's lateness as the forty-eight-hour mark passed and moved into fifty hours. It irritated him, just as every little thing did these days, because he had finally formulated an idea in regards to their travel. While he wanted to continue their course toward the red star, he wanted to carefully watch the space they crossed for anything that could be considered a sign. He was quite certain that the answers he sought were presenting themselves—he just needed to look for them.

At the fifty-two-hour mark, Connor watched from the entry ramp as the crew returned to the ship, smiles on their faces and bounces in their steps. They immediately proceeded to restock the ship's supplies with the platform deliveries Aislinn had arranged, busily moving about the ship and platform until everything had been put into place. Though he should've been grateful for the obvious high-morale, Connor was truly bothered by the crew's disregard of his authority. The sooner they got back to their posts and back under his control, the better he would feel. As soon as the entire crew was back onboard, he went to the command station to make an announcement, something along the lines of Aislinn's suggestion regarding current protocol. He reached over and engaged the intercom.

"Attention all crew, this is Captain Connor. Due to the importance of our current mission, I would like to stress a few points. It is absolutely vital that you carry out all of your post duties to the fullest extent and without exception. If you are unable to do this, please inform your superior immediately. Also, if you observe anything out of the ordinary, you are to report it to your superior immediately. This cannot be stressed enough—anything which is not a normal occurrence must be reported immediately. The penalty for failing to report such abnormalities will be extreme. Lastly, our ability to complete this mission depends on our ability to work smoothly together as a team. As always, I expect your very best performance. Anything less does not belong on this ship, and will be dealt with accordingly. That is all." There, he thought to himself, Captain Leeto could eat his heart out. He felt better, as if a weight had been lifted. And once again, he had a plan.

Chapter 18

The ship jolted suddenly, throwing the two crewmen in the communication room to the floor.

"Jesus Chri— What was that?" Acelin Harrow asked, getting back up to his feet and shaking his head. Haidee Bucket watched as Acelin stretched his long arms, tilting his head and causing his long, light brown hair to fall toward his back. While not entirely good-looking, Acelin did have features that Haidee found attractive, and his hair was one of them.

"It felt like a pocket in the field," Haidee replied, rubbing the back of her neck as she continued to watch Acelin from her spot on the floor. Sharing communication-room duties with Acelin definitely helped, but she was still nervous about being on this ship. After all, if the crew knew that her maiden name had been Leeto, the same name as her younger half-brother, they might suspect her of a hidden agenda. And they'd have been right.

"Comm, control—report," Captain Connor's voice said over the intercom. Acelin pushed the intercom button, leaning close to the communicator.

"Control, comm—identifying," Acelin replied and then released the button and turned to Haidee. "Are you okay?"

"Yeah, probably some bruises, but I'm fine."

"A pocket in the field, eh?" Acelin asked as he moved back over to his workstation. "From what, do you think?"

"I don't know—let's find out," Haidee said, moving over to her workstation and shaking her head at the nonexistent help she received in getting up. She quickly ran her fingers across the panel, pushing buttons and adjusting screens. Acelin was beside her, watching her every move and pretending to help while actually doing nothing. "There's something out ahead of us. Here." She pushed a button to open the screen on the wall, revealing a small asteroid hanging in space in front of them. Or what looked like an asteroid, because it was clearly moving and leaving them to follow in its wake. The ship vibrated again, more gently this time.

"Well, it behaves like a comet, but is darn slow and has no tail," Haidee thought aloud.

"What is it?" Acelin asked.

"I don't know." Haidee's hands continued to move across the control panel. "It's not registering on any of our systems."

"Just a random chunk of inanimate matter free-floating in space?" Acelin's voice was stingingly sarcastic. Haidee knew that Acelin was mocking her since there was no such thing as a random piece of matter. Everything came from somewhere and had a purpose for being where it was.

"Well, that's the weird part," Haidee ignored the sarcasm, "It doesn't scan like inanimate matter."

"Animate matter then?"

"Dormant life, actually. Like it's hibernating."

"Hibernating?" Acelin paused. "A rock? Would you like to tell that to the captain or should I?" Acelin asked.

Haidee turned, glaring angrily at him. "Well, what the heck?"

"Let's not tell him just yet," Haidee suggested, looking at Acelin pointedly. Acelin's eyes opened wide, and he shook his head.

"Oh no, I'm not laying my tail on the line so you can play research scientist. You have no idea what you're dealing with and no authority ..."

"Well, we'll just have to risk it then, won't we?" Haidee interrupted, shrugging. "Maybe we'll just give it a little wake-up call."

"And risk blowing it out of the sky? I think that violates our contact protocol. Remember, if it's alive there's bound to be a hell of a lot of people who will be pissed if you destroy it, and the captain counts as one of them."

"I'm not going to blow it up. I thought I'd just try moving the space near it and see if that draws it out of dormancy."

"Oh yeah, well that oughta make the captain *real* happy." Acelin stood up and backed toward the door. Haidee knew he didn't have the guts to actually report her, but he certainly wouldn't help her. She leaned over and pushed a lever forward on the control panel, listening as the ship purred and emitted a faint ray of energy into space.

"Wow, look at that," Haidee cried, pointing to the screen. The mass before them was glowing and expanding.

"Maybe you should ..." Acelin indicated the communicator.

"Comm, control—neutralize all activities until

further notice," Captain Connor's voice commanded through the communicator before Haidee had a chance to pick it up.

"Shit, he's coming down." Acelin looked around, and Haidee suddenly noticed how messy the room was.

"Copy, control. Comm neutral," Haidee said and put the communicator down, her face blank as she pressed a small series of buttons on the control board.

"What are you doing?" Acelin's voice was shrill. Haidee ignored him and kept typing. "Shit," Acelin said. He glanced over the room again. "Shit."

"Will you stop? There's really nothing to worry about," Haidee said quietly.

"Nothing to worry about? What are you *doing*?" Acelin was obviously nervous, pacing the small room.

"It's the captain, he won't ..." Haidee tried, straightening her hair behind her ears, her heart racing as she continued typing.

"No, the old captain wouldn't maybe. This new captain ..."

"He's still the same captain. He's just ... preoccupied," Haidee said, finishing her typing and throwing her hands into the air in exasperation as she watched her screen fade to black.

"No," Acelin said, shaking his head. "No, he's not the same captain. He's changed somehow. He seems much more impatient and much more interested in having his crew follow every damn code and rule ever devised. When he finds out we were fiddling with a foreign contact—" Acelin stopped, his eyes frozen on the door as it slid open. Captain Connor entered the room with an officer close on his heels.

"Captain Connor," Haidee acknowledged, standing and clasping her hands respectfully behind her back. *Talking about good-looking guys,* she thought to herself. The captain was a fine specimen. He was tall and slender, with just a hint of muscle tone visible through his tight uniform. His dirty blonde hair always seemed slightly disheveled, making him look all the more attractive. His piercing green eyes were breathtaking, and she felt the pangs of regret, longing for things to be different between them. While she had usually felt twinges of remorse for her deceitful actions, the captain before her seemed cold and distant, almost a different person in the same body. *The same gorgeous body,* she thought to herself quietly.

Acelin stepped next to Haidee, bumping her slightly. Sweat beaded on his forehead as he saluted formally. "Captain."

"Where is the contact?" Connor moved to the small screen against the wall, seemingly oblivious to the tangible tension in the room.

"Here, sir." Haidee pressed a button and indicated the object filling the screen, now quite noticeably glowing from within.

"Responses to comm initiation?" Connor asked, turning to Acelin.

"The contact seemed to expand and glow in response to radar pulsing, Captain," Acelin responded, and Haidee noted that he was struggling to keep his eyes on Captain Connor's. What a wimp.

"Who initiated comm with contact?" Connor's voice was soft.

"She did!" Acelin nearly shouted, pointing at her. Haidee rolled her eyes—the man had absolutely no nerve at all. Couldn't step up to do something bold but had no problem ratting her out to the captain. Captain Connor's eyes moved to hers, and she nodded once in confirmation. Captain Connor remained quiet for a moment longer and then turned suddenly, indicating to the officer that had come with him.

"Officer Devlin, what is the standard procedure when identifying a foreign contact in the field?"

"Notify control, Captain," Devlin responded curtly.

"Why is that, Officer?"

"So that any potential threats to the ship and information important to the mission can be identified and analyzed immediately by the proper crew, Captain."

"And wherein lies the fault and danger in failing to identify foreign contacts and initiating any sort of communication without control's knowledge and instruction?" Connor asked. Acelin looked as though he needed to go to the bathroom.

"The contact could perceive such initiation to be a hostile act, Captain," Devlin answered, "and our uninformed crew would be unprepared to counter such a hostile act."

"Thank you, Officer. Bring Balin and Ada up for duty in comm. Dismissed." Officer Devlin nodded and left the room. Connor turned slowly toward Haidee and Acelin. "This mission, more than any other, depends entirely on reading all contacts that we encounter.

Failure to report all contacts and initiating communication yourself without control authorization will not only jeopardize the mission itself but also potentially endanger the ship and the entire crew. Any justifications you may have for your actions will not outweigh the faults that lie in the actions themselves. You are to report for duty in the officers' mess and will apply to me for release from said duty. Understood?"

"Yes, Captain," they replied simultaneously.

"Dismissed," Connor said. Haidee watched Acelin bow his head in shame as he stepped through the door. She followed, feeling just a little bit of guilt.

***

Connor sighed deeply, his eyes turning back to the object on the screen. "Damn," he whispered. There was something important about this rock, he just knew it. It was something he was meant to remember and understand, but his mind remained blank. The door to the comm room slid open, and he nodded as Balin and Ada entered the room.

"On duty, Captain," Balin said as he moved to the communication panel, his short legs and arms requiring him to adjust his seat and the control board before him. Ada sat down in the second chair, pushing her long black hair over her shoulders and pursing her lips as if to concentrate.

"There is an unidentified contact in the field. Identify the contact and initiate communication," Connor said.

"Aye," Ada said, angling her long neck toward Connor by way of salute before busily pressing buttons. After a few moments, the screen shrunk. "Contact appears to be dormant, Captain, though it is responding to our radar pulsing by glowing."

"Is there any energy being generated outwardly from the contact?" Connor asked.

"No, Captain. The energy seems centered within itself. Our contact fields are being stored as energy, causing the matter to … expand," Balin said.

Connor reached for the communicator and pulled it to his mouth. "Control, comm—this is the captain. Stop all engines and hold."

"Comm, control—ship holding, Captain," Aislinn's voice said over the communicator.

Balin and Ada steadied themselves with the communication panel as the ship slowed and stopped. The object on the screen that they had approached and nearly overtaken maintained a slow rate of speed and now moved slowly away from them. If it was a thinking life form and knew the ship had stopped, it certainly wasn't indicating any alarm or concern. Connor knew that unless they could identify it somehow, they may as well have missed it altogether.

"Captain, we have a positive identification match," Balin said.

Connor stepped behind him. "Display," Connor said impatiently. The screen cleared and then filled with an entry.

"It is a Kalyca—a 'rosebud' in space," Balin read aloud, his voice betraying a note of wonder. "Astrologists believe that it is part of the matter that was originally expanding and contracting in the universe's creation. It was likely displaced prior to condensing into a formed star or planet, and it has never picked up enough energy from gravity pulls to move into a comet-like orbit. No one is sure why, but it has some lifelike properties in that it grabs and stores energy."

"Are you aware of any other Kalycas in this particular galaxy?" Connor asked.

"Yes, Captain, there is one at the outer edge of the galaxy," Ada said, pointing to her screen. The screen showed the outside edge of a galaxy that looked remarkably familiar to Connor. Ada's finger was just below a spot on the screen that was marked with a blue dot.

"Control, comm—this is the captain," Connor said into the communicator, his eyes on the blue dot.

"Comm, control," Aislinn's voice replied.

"Comm is sending coordinates for another location within this galaxy. Please set a direct course."

"Yes, Captain."

"Oh, my god," Ada said, her fingers racing across the control panel as her screen flashed to black.

"Yes?" Connor turned.

"The Kalyca is gone." She indicated to the screen, showing only black before the ship where the Kalyca had been only minutes earlier.

Connor smiled, pulling his notebook and pen from his pocket. "Never mind. Give the coordinates for the galaxy's other Kalyca to control. I'll contact you from there."

"Yes, Captain."

Chapter 19

Her heart quickened as she approached the garden. Her hair blew back in the gentle breeze, revealing her glowing face. Her eyes sparkled with excitement as she straightened her dress and brushed out the wrinkles. She stood near the bench for two minutes, excitement turned to concern even though she realized she was early. Another two minutes and her eyes fell to her feet, matching her emotion. He wasn't coming, something whispered inside herself. No, she answered boldly, raising her eyes in time to see him approaching, his body a tall testament to physical strength. A small smile formed at the center of her lips and then grew, widening from ear to ear. His last few steps were nearly a jog, and then he swept her into his strong arms, twirling her around and breathing his warm breath into her porcelain ear. She relaxed, allowing herself to give in to him completely.

The Kalyca at the edge of the galaxy was considerably smaller than the one they had encountered several days earlier. Not knowing what else to do, Connor had the ship remain hovering before the Kalyca. The crew quickly grew restless, and Connor grew nervous. The command station was almost humid, and Connor watched as Aislinn wiped beaded sweat off her forehead and rubbed her neck.

"What's wrong, Aislinn?" Connor's voice was edged with concern. Unlike the other crew in the command station, she took few breaks and was beginning to look rather burnt out, her face paler than normal. His voice must have been louder than he'd intended, as several crew turned from their stations to look at Aislinn.

"Oh, I just … my throat's a little sore, that's all," Aislinn said, waving the crew back to work.

"Maybe you should report to the sickbay and have that checked out," Connor suggested.

"It's not painful—it's just from voice overuse, that's all. It should abate on its own if I just rest it today."

"You sure?" Connor was maintaining some distance from her, not so sure she was simply suffering from the beginnings of voice loss.

"Yes, Captain, it's fine," Aislinn replied.

"Fine," Connor acknowledged, though he still maintained his distance. "While we wait, I'd like to get an updated course for the red star in the Lena System."

"Very well, Captain," Aislinn replied, moving her hands over the console. Connor watched the screen as it pinpointed their location and destination and then cut a path through the infinite. "Captain?" Aislinn turned, her hands formally crossed behind her back. Connor nodded, his eyes following the lines on the screen. Aislinn's body lurched slightly with the force of a small cough. Connor's eyes met hers, and he noticed they were watery.

"Are you sure you're okay?" he asked. Aislinn nodded, patting her chest lightly. Connor looked back at the map. "What is this, here?" he asked, his fingers following a detour indicated on the map. "Why the sudden triangle off course?"

"There is a dense asteroid belt here," Aislinn pointed to the area their course avoided. "It's a bit too treacherous for this ship to navigate, so the computer programmed a path around it," she coughed again, harder.

"Is there a long time delay?" Connor asked as Aislinn caught her breath.

"Maybe ten hours," Aislinn answered, still coughing.

"Ten hours?" Connor questioned

"Yes, Captain," Aislinn replied before being overtaken by violent coughing. A pause for breath brought on another fit, and her face began to turn a shade of violet.

"Aislinn," Connor began as Aislinn once again attempted to catch her breath. He paused when she began coughing again. "You must report to sickbay immediately," he finished when she was done.

"Captain …" Aislinn argued between coughs.

"Immediately!" Connor snapped. The command station echoed and fell silent.

"Yes, Captain," Aislinn replied, turning and walking to the door of the command station. As she reached her arm up to open the door, she began coughing again, violently, and held herself up with a nearby console as she gasped for air. The crew remained silent and still. Connor turned, indicating to a young man sitting at the command station's communications console.

"Travis, get sick bay here—now," Connor ordered.

"Aye," Travis replied. He turned, pressed a button, and spoke into his mouthpiece. "Control to sickbay—we need a quarantine pod immediately."

"Copy," a voice replied. Aislinn had finally caught her breath, but she was gasping and shaking. Connor looked intently at her, as if to ask whether she was okay. Aislinn nodded, her voice rasping in her throat with every breath.

Doctor Simon appeared suddenly in the open doorway to the command station, and Connor wondered how he had made it up from the sickbay so fast. Doctor Simon's graying hair and wrinkled face indicated he was middle aged, and his short, stocky frame did not convey an image of speedy movement. Connor decided the doctor must have been nearby when he heard the call. Doctor Simon had a small hoop in his hand, and he quickly placed it on the ground around Aislinn. It immediately sprang up, encasing her in a small pod. Doctor Simon then pulled a small scanner out of his belt and held it before the pod. It beeped loudly as it scanned the pod.

"What is it?" Connor asked.

"At first glance it appears to be a respiratory virus," Doctor Simon replied, "but it is quite unlike any I've ever seen before. It appears to be emanating from her heart rather than her lungs."

"Is it …" Connor covered his mouth with his hand. While he'd never been fond of vitamins, Connor was terrified of all illnesses and had always thought it was best if people quarantined themselves in their private homes until they were better.

"I'm not sure. Until I find out, I recommend a safety evacuation of all decks."

"Emergency crew, don your quarantine uniforms and take your emergency posts," Connor immediately said to the command station crew. "The rest of you, place your stations in hold and clear the deck. Remain in your quarters until further notice from me." He nodded to Travis. "Give me an all systems page." Travis flipped a switch. "Crew of the *Scarlet Tarika*, this is the captain. A crewmember has been infected by a respiratory illness. Until the illness is contained and it is deemed safe to move about the ship, I ask that all crewmembers place their stations on hold and retire to their quarters. Once again, this is the captain asking all crew to retire to their quarters until further notice." He nodded to Travis, who flipped the intercom off and left the room.

"You should get to your own quarters, Captain," Doctor Simon said. "This virus may be airborne." Connor nodded and turned to leave.

"Can you—" He paused, turning back to Doctor Simon. "You *can* cure it, right?"

"I will try," Doctor Simon said, nodding. Connor managed a weak smile at Aislinn before he turned and left.

Chapter 20

She was nearly there. At long last she could see the light at the end of the darkness. And yet, for as close as she was now, she didn't know if she could make it the last little bit. She was tired, she was weak, and there was still a long ways to go. But the light was there now, defining the end of the dark struggle, and she knew she would push on until she couldn't anymore.

Connor was awoken from his brief nap by the annoying buzz of his communicator. He rolled over and shook his head, trying to fully wake up.

"Yes?" he rasped into the communicator, coughing to clear his throat.

"Captain, this is Doctor Simon."

"Yes, Doctor."

"I have a diagnosis on Officer Aislinn if you'd like to come down to sickbay."

"I'll be right there." Connor sat up and slipped his shoes on, running his fingers through his hair as he stepped out into the corridor. Within minutes he was in the sickbay, standing over Aislinn's bed next to Doctor Simon. Connor eyed Aislinn thoughtfully and was sure her face was becoming ashen before his very eyes. Despite this, her blue eyes and full, red lips stood out beautifully, and Connor couldn't help thinking she still looked stunning.

"Are you going to be sick?" Connor asked when Aislinn clutched at her stomach.

"No," Aislinn said, but Connor thought she only sounded half certain. "Yes," she decided, sitting up and placing her hand over her mouth.

"Don't worry, there's nothing in your stomach," Doctor Simon soothed, rubbing Aislinn gently on her back. Aislinn nodded, her hand still over her mouth as she made uncomfortable faces. She shivered, and perspiration soaked through the back of her gown. After a moment she coughed, continuing to keep her hand over her mouth.

"Perhaps we should …" Doctor Simon indicated to the door. Connor nodded.

"She needs her rest, I agree." Connor placed his hand gently over Aislinn's. "Get better," he added. Aislinn nodded, smiling weakly. Connor stepped out into the corridor behind Doctor Simon.

"Captain," Doctor Simon began.

"Have you identified the illness?" Connor asked. Doctor Simon shrugged helplessly.

"Not with absolute certainty, Captain." Connor raised his eyebrows. Doctor Simon cleared his throat. "I ran some preliminary tests to determine any imbalances or abnormalities in her system." He paused, looking back toward Aislinn to be sure she couldn't hear him.

"Yes, and?" Connor asked impatiently.

"Realize, Captain, that without an imbalance or any infection to test, I cannot determine what the infection or illness is."

"I'm sorry, I'm not sure I understand." Connor rubbed his forehead with his index finger. "You're saying there's nothing wrong with her?"

"All of her tests are reading normal," Doctor Simon responded.

"But if that's so, Doctor, then why is she still so weak?"

"As far as the tests are concerned, there is nothing wrong with her. However, that is not the same thing she is telling herself. In her own mind, she is very ill."

"She is? Very ill?" Connor paused. "You're telling me that she is imagining this illness, like some crooked game of make believe?"

"There are no objective findings to justify her current symptoms," Doctor Simon said, rubbing his chin in perplexity. "She complains of headaches and a chill, indicative of a high fever, but her body temperature is normal. She goes through all the motions and violent retching of a flu, but there is no infection, nor indeed is there any stomach content, to justify this. All of her symptoms are psychosomatic, self-generated, but they aren't carrying through to real physical markers."

"I assume it follows that the illness is not contagious?" Connor realized he was only concerned about himself—he wanted to ensure that he would not get ill. Doctor Simon frowned.

"I'm afraid there is still some danger, Captain. As Aislinn has demonstrated, the mind can be quite convincing. If the crew believes she is truly ill and that they too can become ill, they very well could end up in the sickbay right beside her. And the more that the crew believe it, the more deadly diseases like this can become." Doctor Simon's voice was solemn. Connor thought of the Salem witch trials, of how many innocent lives were wasted because of fictitious accusations. Could the same thing occur here, medically?

"Keep me informed of her progress," Connor said suddenly.

"I will, Captain," Doctor Simon replied, turning back toward the infirmary room.

"One thing, Doctor," Connor said. Doctor Simon turned, eyeing Connor attentively.

"You said 'diseases like this' … Can I take that to mean you've seen symptoms similar to this before?"

"Just once, Captain," Doctor Simon said.

"What happened?" Connor asked. Doctor Simon closed the infirmary door, his face solemn.

"The crew perished—all save fifteen men," Doctor Simon shivered involuntarily.

"What was the disease called?" Connor asked.

"They called it Marjeta," Doctor Simon replied.

"Marjeta?" Connor repeated, his pen and notebook in hand.

"It means 'Hidden Pearl,'" Doctor Simon said. "It was more powerful than any illness I'd ever heard of before." He ran his hand through his hair as he reminisced. "Crew were infected instantaneously upon hearing of another's distress and would scream about symptoms they didn't have until suddenly those symptoms appeared. The fifteen who survived were asleep during the epidemic and awoke to find their crewmembers dead without apparent reason. The medical logs were confusing and gave little insight into the disease or how it affected the men." Doctor Simon's voice was low, and Connor felt a shiver creep up his spine.

"What can you do for her?" Connor asked, replacing his pen and notebook in his pocket.

"I truly feel there's only one thing I *can* do," Doctor Simon said matter-of-factly. "Give her placebos while convincing her that she's been given a cure of some sort." Connor nodded.

"And that will work?"

"If this truly is the psychosomatic illness it appears to be, yes, that should work."

"Okay. Please keep me updated if anything changes," Connor said.

"Absolutely, Captain."

Chapter 21

The trees, once stark and empty, showed off small buds of color. It marked the end of a long, harsh winter and the beginning of warmth and new life. That's what it meant to him as well—new life.

Doctor Simon's placebo worked quickly, and two days later Aislinn was given medical approval to return to her station. Connor had been waiting anxiously, for without her in the command station he had felt uncertain about giving new orders regarding their travel plans. The morning of Aislinn's return, Connor felt as excited as a kid going to Disneyland. He dressed quickly and eagerly, and he had to struggle not to break out and run down the corridor to the command station.

"Welcome back, Aislinn," Connor said as he entered the room. Aislinn looked up from her station and smiled warmly. Connor noticed her cheeks were rosy with healthy color, and her eyes were bright with energy and life. It was a great improvement, and seeing it made Connor realize how much he had worried for her.

"Thank you, Captain."

"Feeling better?" Connor asked politely.

"Yes, Captain, so much better," Aislinn answered.

"I'm glad to hear it. It was a bit ... strange not having you around." Connor suppressed a grimace—did that come out as flirtatious as when he played it back in his mind?

"Thank you, Captain," Aislinn said, smiling again and

pushing her hair out of her eyes. "I'm ready to proceed, if there are any directions you want to …" She paused, letting her unfinished sentence dangle in the air.

"Please find the Marjeta System," Connor said. He didn't even bother to control the excitement in his voice.

"The Marjeta System, Captain?"

"Yes."

"I haven't heard of such a system, Captain," Aislinn said, her blue eyes sparkling with what Connor assumed was curiosity.

"Does that mean it doesn't exist?" Connor asked, raising his eyebrow inquisitively. His excitement did nothing to weaken the sensation he felt whenever he looked at Aislinn. It was like a ghostly shadow passing through his body, turning his body heat up a few degrees.

"No, Captain. I'll run a search," Aislinn said quickly.

"Thank you, Aislinn," Connor replied, taking a seat in his chair.

"Captain, I'm not finding a Marjeta System," Aislinn said from her console a few moments later. Connor leaned forward, squinting to see the screen. "However, I have found a star named Maiden Pearl," she added, turning to look at him. His heart quickened.

"Maiden Pearl?"

"Yes, Captain, it's in the Friar Galaxy," Aislinn said, enlarging the map for Connor to see.

"How far away is that?" Connor asked, studying the map.

"It's approximately two days from here, Captain."

"Set a course for the Maiden Pearl," Connor said,

sliding back into his chair. "And program the computer to pick up any anomalies along the way."

"Yes, Captain," Aislinn said, programming the coordinates into the computer. There was the echoing of commands as their new course was sent to the work stations and the crew set to work.

Chapter 22

I found it, *he said quietly to himself, scarcely daring to believe it. He had spent so many long hours searching and calculating, and he had often considered giving up. But now he had finally found the answer he needed, the one that would solve everything and allow him a fresh start. The thought built, and he felt the adrenaline pumping through his body. Finally, he thought,* I found *it.*

The Maiden Pearl was the first star Connor had seen up close since he'd last seen the Sun from Earth. The Maiden Pearl's system was easily four times the size of Earth's solar system, and the star itself was at least fifty times bigger than the Sun. Connor stared out the command station window at the planets that faithfully rotated around their star. Despite obvious differences between the Maiden Pearl System and the Earth's solar system, Connor still felt a sting of familiarity when looking at it.

"Captain, we have located the galaxy's black hole," Aislinn announced, pulling up the star screen and causing it to focus on the galactic center point, where light seemed to disappear. "Would you like us to set a course?" She turned and faced him, her eyes glowing.

Connor looked at the star screen and felt the weight of his answer even before it was spoken. "No, the anomaly isn't there." He turned away from Aislinn and began pacing, thinking. As a general rule, black holes existed at the center of every galaxy, with one very notable exception. If they were seeking the antithesis of the Black Hole

Brigade, they needed to look for an exception to the rule. They needed to look …

"Officer Aislinn, can you run a diagnostic on the space around the Friar Galaxy?" Connor asked, turning back to Aislinn. She nodded, but he saw the question in her eyes.

"Yes, Captain." She nodded to several crew who had turned to her for instruction and now turned back to their workstations. Aislinn moved closer to Connor. "Captain?" she questioned.

"Trust me," Connor breathed quietly near her ear, his voice only loud enough for her to hear him. She nodded, and he heard her breath quicken.

"Captain, there's something here," a crewman said suddenly, standing at his station. He was young and excited, bobbing his head of red curls gently as he waited for Connor and Aislinn to approach his station.

"What is it?" Connor asked, pressing forward. "Can you bring it up on the star screen?" The crewman bobbed his head again, pushing several buttons. The star screen became dark, but it was not entirely black. There was one corner of the screen that seemed to glow faintly. Connor's breath caught in his throat.

"That's it," he said quietly. Then louder, "That's it!" He paused, feeling the eyes of the crew on him. "Aislinn, put us on an intercept course with the anomaly," Connor said, walking back to his command chair on the bridge. Aislinn nodded slightly.

"Yes, Captain." She quickly delegated the coordinate programming to her juniors and joined Connor on the bridge.

"Captain, there is something you should know." Aislinn's voice was low, secretive. Aislinn stepped closer, and Connor smelled the warm, vanilla-sugar scent he had grown so fond of.

"Yes?" Connor responded quietly.

"This black hole, it's ..." Aislinn paused again, searching for words.

"Yes?" Connor urged, appreciating the sweet smell of her breath.

"Its properties identify it as ... it's the same as the one ... the last time ..." Aislinn struggled and then shrugged helplessly. Connor nodded and spoke the words for her.

"It's the same one we encountered before?" He knew the answer was true, even before Aislinn nodded. "Well, that's good, right?" Connor asked. Aislinn shrugged again, though slightly.

"Hard to say, Captain—this has never happened before. I mean, to collapse as it did before and then reappear in an entirely different system ... we really have no prior experience to explain that or to explain what we may expect this time."

"Are you afraid?" Connor asked quietly.

"No," Aislinn replied in whisper.

"Not just a little bit?"

"No," she said a little more quickly.

"What are you afraid of?" Connor pressed. He could see she was reluctant, as though she was worried her concerns would not be well received.

"Just the unknown," she said decisively. Connor nodded.

"The great unknown, that makes sense," he said. "Many people are afraid of what they can't be sure of."

"Well, it's not that so much as ..." Aislinn stopped short. Connor watched her, his face eagerly urging her to continue. She smiled and opened her mouth to continue, "What if this is it? What if there's nothing more to this? Have I done everything I wanted to? Is there anything I will regret leaving without? I just don't like losing the element of control."

"Or what if this isn't it?" Connor asked matter-of-factly.

"Then I have nothing to worry about—anything I've forgotten up until now I can rectify. It's what I might not have done and will have no time to change that ..." She stopped again as if searching for the right words.

"Scares you?" Connor tried.

"Worries me," Aislinn corrected.

"Well, if there's nothing you'll be able to do about it, why worry about it? Why not just assume that you've done everything you've wanted and you've left nothing behind? Then at least you'll get through it with an easy stomach," Connor shrugged.

"It sounds so easy, but I can't help thinking." Aislinn's eyes remained distant.

"Then I'll just have to keep you busy." Connor handed her a communicator and indicated to the door. "Make sure all the systems are ready for the interception. If we can make it through the anomaly, we'll need to do it with a secure ship."

"Yes, Captain." Aislinn nodded, took the communicator, and walked out the door.

Connor smiled. He knew he was close now.

***

"Captain," Connor's communicator buzzed. He was sitting alone in his quarters, toying with nervous excitement as he watched a desk clock tick each second away.

"Yes, Aislinn?" Connor responded.

"We have activity," Aislinn said mysteriously.

"I'll be right there," Connor said, moving out of the room and down the corridor to the command station. The room was deathly quiet, more so than usual. "What is it? Why are you all so quiet?" Connor asked as he approached his seat and sat down.

"Captain, we're nearly there. Are you sure ..." Aislinn began. She coughed and fell quiet.

"Nearly to the anomaly?" Connor asked, glancing up at the screen. "Let me see it," he ordered. Aislinn nodded to a crewmember. A small motion dissolved the star screen, and the command station window revealed vast space. Just before them, playing with light in a way that tricked the eye (was it absorbing light or emitting it?), was the black hole.

"Captain ..." Aislinn tried again, swallowing. Connor watched her face and saw the beads of sweat forming on her forehead.

"What is it, Aislinn?"

"Captain, our first ship ..." Aislinn stopped again.

"Yes, our first ship. We lost it just like this," Connor acknowledged quietly. He stood and cleared his throat to address the crew. "I understand you all feel ... uncomfortable to be back in this situation," he said loudly, "but

I'm anxious for some answers, and I know you must be too. We know nothing—we have nowhere to begin. We lost our first ship this way, that's all we know. Our ship …" He paused, desperately trying to remember. "What was it," he said quietly toward Aislinn.

"The Keir Abrienda, Captain," Aislinn whispered. The crew fell dead silent, and all movement stopped.

"The Keir Abrienda?" Connor muttered as he looked up at the flight screen and the small words written across the bottom. His mind screamed at him—his first ship was named after the very anomaly that destroyed it and the one that sat before them even now? Even he, who was looking for clues and answers, found that a bit too creepy. As panic and uncertainty began to seize him, the ship began to shake, fighting an invisible force that was pulling it in.

"Captain!" a crewman called out, and Connor rushed to the man's station with Aislinn at his heels.

"What is it?"

"It's *Journey*," the rather chubby crewman said, indicating to the screen and a small, red dot on it. Aislinn and Connor exchanged looks. "Captain Leeto must have tracked us here somehow—he's nearing the event horizon," the crewman said, waving a short, fat finger at his screen.

"Shall we hold?" Aislinn asked. Connor shook his head.

"No, we're going in," Connor said firmly. "Leeto wants to beat us there and take the credit, and for once I'm not going to sit back and let it happen."

The crew sprung into action, flipping switches and

turning levers. With the same certainty that he knew it was too late, Connor knew they had lost their nerve and were trying to pull back from the event horizon against his orders. He stood still, holding onto the edge of the platform as the ship shuddered and fell silent—and moved forward steadily. All motion on the bridge stopped as the crew became statues, transfixed by the sight before them.

The spherical surface of the black hole moved and spun as though alive. All of the light that passed so easily into the event horizon seemed to absorb slowly into the center of the black hole only to be shot out again infinitely fast. The edges of the sphere trapped the light, however, spinning it back to the center to begin again on a loop it would never escape from. The resulting light show was unlike anything Connor could have dreamed and made the northern lights he'd once seen in Minnesota appear a cheap parlor trick of flashlights. Connor also knew this very event was impossible according to black-hole research scientists. Unless the black hole was reversing its gravity pull outwards, it was impossible to see anything past the event horizon.

"Seven seconds to singularity, Captain," someone said dully. Connor nodded, acknowledging the death-countdown. He could feel the pulling, the invisible and supremely powerful gravitational force of the black hole. Something touched his hand, and he glanced down to see Aislinn holding his hand firmly with hers. He looked up, his eyes meeting hers, and he suddenly felt that everything was perfect. So perfect, he thought, it was almost as though … *as though I'd written it.* Connor's breath caught in his throat, and for a long moment he stood frozen in place. As if it were an afterthought, Connor extracted the notebook from his pocket and flipped it back to the beginning, quickly scanning through until the end. His breath came in short gasps now, excitement pounding through his veins as he recalled when he'd first met Basha—mere moments after deciding he needed a muse. Every time he felt bored, he was truly and deeply bored. Every time he felt a rush of excitement, something exciting happened onboard. And then there was Aislinn, the embodiment of his perfect woman. And, of course, there was Captain Leeto—always pushing Connor and making him feel both inspired and insufficient. Captain Leeto, who reminded him of … Connor let out a gasp.

Connor's writing professor at night college had been a young man named Lee Tobin. Actually, "young" was an understatement—Lee was practically a baby. He was a prodigy child, earning a GED when he was twelve years old and graduating from college when he was sixteen. No amount of smarts, however, could erase the immaturity that held strong in every adolescent, and Lee was cocky as all hell. At eighteen years old, the professor was a completely arrogant ass, demanding the best from every student but claiming they could never be as good as he was. For all his posturing, Lee's own experience was superficial at best. He had written over fifty articles and five novellas, most of them regarding global warming theories. Every single one had been rejected on the premise that it was all theory and conjecture, and weak at that. The college had only accepted him in the position of a night-class professor because they were financially barren. Child prodigy that he was, Lee brought attention, and therefore money, to the college. As a professor he was as weak as his own writing, encouraging only rarely and always insincerely. Connor had watched student after student drop out, either to pursue other dreams or to just give up entirely. Connor was incredibly strong willed and stayed in, his one goal being to get out and prove Lee wrong by really making it as a writer. Lee had dared him, practically sneering as he promised that Connor's writing would never amount to anything more than a hobby.

Connor smiled as he finally confronted the truth. The power to write, to change his world, lay in his hands and his alone. It always had.

Connor sighed deeply, relaxing as he realized what he needed to do. A loud shout grabbed his attention, and he turned his eyes toward the window as a blinding flash lit the sky. Captain Connor smiled as he fell back into his chair, immediately knocked senseless from the blast. One last thought lingered into the darkness.

Connor was Celtic, and it meant strong willed.

Chapter 23

At the very top of the cliff, he pulled hard with his aching arms and swung a leg over the top, pulling himself up. He stood slowly, his breath laboring in the thin air as he looked out over the valley below. It had all been worth it—every scrape, every burning muscle. It had all been worth it. For this.

Connor shifted in the bed, trying to escape the pitiful whimpering that seemed to be coming from within his ears. With his movement the sound paused, only to start up louder than it had been before. Connor shifted again, moving his arms to push the noise away. Again it paused and was immediately followed by a sharp yap. Connor opened his eyes, smiling at the puppy that sat next to him on the bed.

"Hello, Ralph," Connor said roughly. Ralph yapped in answer, jumping forward and licking Connor's face. "Ugh … hold on, here …" Connor said, pushing Ralph off his chest and stepping onto the cold, wood floor. He carefully made his way to the bathroom with his eyes half closed. He turned on the faucet, his hands sticking uncomfortably to the knobs. He pulled them away, put his hands under the water, and splashed his face. The phone rang loudly, each ring followed by a sharp yap from Ralph. Connor turned the water off and grabbed a dry washcloth as he moved into the kitchen. He pulled the phone from the cradle, sat down heavily in his chair, and put the phone to his ear.

"Hello?" Connor croaked. Water, where was that glass of water? He looked around the kitchen, spying the glass on the counter. He stood and moved to retrieve it, taking a long gulp.

"Connor?" an excited voice asked.

"Yeah," Connor said, his voice still scratchy.

"Connor! My man! I got your e-mail—I'll be on you later to find out where you got a computer—but this is great! When can I see the whole thing?" the voice exploded, ringing in Connor's ears.

"Huh?" Connor asked, rubbing the sleep out of his eyes.

"I can't believe you put me through all that shit the other day. Writer's block—hah! I should be so lucky to have your writer's block. When can I get the full manuscript?" the voice asked. Connor's mind wandered, trying to place the voice. It finally clicked. It was Jim, his agent/editor.

"Jim?" Connor asked.

"That's me!" Jim replied. "You okay, man?"

"When did I get back from the hospital?" Connor asked, his hand closing on a small bottle in his pocket.

"The hospital? Dude, that was days ago! Okay, you seriously need to wake up, man. This is a big day and you're completely out of it." Jim sounded mildly irritated.

"I, uh …" Connor stopped, rubbing his hand across his head, surprised at what he felt. Or rather, what he didn't feel. There was nothing there, not even the mild discomfort of a small bruise. "I guess I finally got a good night's sleep." Connor's eyes fell on the atomic clock on the wall. November 13th—just five days after he had met … "Basha," Connor said quietly.

"What now?" Jim asked, static coming over the line.

"Sorry," Connor explained. He glanced down at the small bottle in his hand, now only half full of the yellow drops. "I took some of those pills you recommended. Guess they knocked me out pretty good."

"What pills?"

"You know—those vitamins you gave me?"

"You mean the lemon drops in the fake vitamin bottle?" Jim laughed.

"Whaddaya mean?" Connor asked, rubbing his face.

"What's happening over there? Seriously, after all you put me through a week ago, I should be entitled to some explanations myself. I mean, man! Aren't you excited?"

"Excited?" Connor put his elbow on the desk, catching himself as it slid forward across a pile of paper. "I …" He stopped, glancing at the disorganized heap of paper under his arm.

"I'm telling you, this is really great!" Jim exclaimed over the phone. Connor barely heard him. His eyes ran over the large words typed on the sheet in front of him.

"*A Journey Forgotten*," Connor read aloud. He flipped through the sheaf of papers, his eyes grazing over the passages.

"Great title," Jim acknowledged.

"Oh my god, it's my … it's …" Connor choked on his words. How was this possible? Had he been writing in his sleep?

"It's a hit, that's what it is. You're obviously not awake yet, probably stayed up all night partying when you finished it. Why don't you shower, eat some breakfast, and get the full manuscript over to Aislinn by noon." Connor's heart stopped.

"Aislinn?" Connor asked quietly.

"Yeah, you know—my new receptionist? Geez, man, I've told you about her—I've been trying to get you two to meet 'cause I really think you'd hit it off. Oh, man, she's gorgeous, too. Long legs, dark hair, blue eyes—a real stunner. Should be modeling instead of working for a schmuck like me. Totally your type and then some. A real smooth talker too. She's convinced me to hire a friend of hers even though goodness knows I don't have enough for her to do, let alone a whole other person. Another unique name—mothers must've been friends—she's a transplant from Atlanta. Oh, what is it … ah! Basha! Hey, you should bring the manuscript around yourself. Then we can all have lunch together," Jim's voice clearly portrayed his excitement. "We'll go full throttle on this one, man—the works. Call me when you're awake, okay?" Jim asked.

"Yeah," Connor said, dropping the phone onto the table. He flipped through the manuscript again, his eyes blurring over the words as he skimmed from beginning to end. "It's all here," he said aloud, a smile creeping onto his face. "I can't … believe it." He stood up, his gaze never breaking from the huge stack of papers on the table.

Was it really a dream? he wondered, rubbing his forehead carefully. Had it all been a dream? He nodded as if to answer himself. Maybe it had been. But then, how had the entire trip ended up on the papers before him? How had he written a complete novel in five days' time?

He'd always believed a good book wrote itself, but this … this was a miracle.

His eyes fell on a familiar book sitting on the corner of the table. He smiled. It was a book on space travel he had checked out from the library some time ago. He flipped through the first few pages and was only mildly surprised to see an artist's rendering of a ship named the *Scarlet Tarika* on a page discussing intergalactic travel. As he pushed the open book onto the table, something crackled, and Connor spotted a small scrap of paper pushed into the binding. He unfolded it carefully and stared at his scrawled handwriting, a smile lighting his face.

Aislinn = inspiration.